I0598915

LOS HUESOS

A Novel by Izaak David Diggs

ISBN 978-1-7345428-9-9

Cover photograph by Ike James

Official release 28 June, 2022

1

(2008)

How had such a beautiful place become so sad? The old man took a sip of coffee as he stared at the flowers growing just past the edge of the patio. *She* had planted those; everytime he looked at the flowers he thought of her...she was gone but the flowers still lived. He had contemplated tearing them out but wasn't sure which was worse: Being reminded of losing his wife every time he saw the flowers or having her presence in their home diminish even further. The man had already donated her clothes, even her perfumes, to the servants and their friends. Initially, it had made it easier, not seeing and smelling those things of hers day to day, but the old man had come to miss them, those remaining traces of his wife—

The flowers would stay...for the time being.

After finishing his coffee the old man took his cup to the kitchen and set it on the counter. A young woman in a simple, light blue dress was making out a grocery list at a table under a window. Hearing the old man walk in, the woman looked up at him with a smile.

"You could have left your cup on the patio, Don Hector," she said, pausing before adding, "Let me take care of you."

Let me take care of you.

It had been eight months since Esmerelda's passing and they were still treating him like a fragile object. Cecilia meant well; Hector understood that and forced a smile as he had forced many smiles over eight months.

"I do not mind," the old man said. "I like doing things."

She went back to pondering the shopping list.

"Are you hungry?" Cecilia asked, adding something to the list.

"Not yet, thank you."

He looked up at a copper pan hanging from a hook and remembered when he and Esmerelda had found it in a shop: She had fallen in love with it---he had been doubtful about what seemed an impractical pot and they had gone back and forth in that little *tienda* until he had relented. The flowers were hers, the pot was hers...he had to look away.

"I'll be in my study," he said.

Cecilia looked over at him with a smile and nod and then went back to her list.

Hector went to his computer and got online to read the news: The recession was still very bad up north. The *norteamericanos* had elected a black man as their president---

A knock on the door to his study startled him. It was a smiling man in his mid-thirties: Jet black hair, face too plain to be handsome, low key but expensive clothes. Hector smiled and rose from his chair.

"Nieto!" He said.

"Buenos días, abuelo," the younger man smiled.

The two men embraced, Hector gestured to the couch and both men sat on opposite ends facing each other.

"Can I have Cecilia bring you some coffee?" The grandfather asked.

"No, I am fine," the younger man said. "Did you hear about Mr. Obama?"

"Yes. Maybe there is hope for the north, yet."

His grandson laughed a little but then his face became sad.

"I did not go to the hospital this morning," he said softly.

"Yesterday...something bad happened."

"What, nieto?" Hector asked, his own face full of concern.

The younger man was trying to be strong but his grandfather could tell he was wrestling with painful things---

"Did someone die, Rueben?" The older man inquired softly.

4

Reuben nodded, he was staring across the room at a painting of a small *pueblo* but not seeing it.

"It was so stupid, abuelo: A ruptured appendix---who dies from that these days?"

"How did it happen?"

Hector felt bad for his grandson but he also worried: Reuben always became distraught when a patient died even after several years as a doctor. The older man wanted to be stern with his grandson, remind him that he needed to develop a thicker skin, but he also loved his *nieto* and did not want to be harsh with him when the young man was already hurting.

"This man ignored the pain for three days," Reuben looked at his grandfather incredulously. "How do you ignore something like that for so long?"

"*No se,*" the older man sighed.

But he did: Some men like to play the tough guy, do not want to admit they are helpless and need care—sometimes they die for their *machismo*.

"I know I need to not let these things bother me," the younger man sighed. "How long did it take you to get used to death, abuelo?"

Hector looked across the room at the painting, remembering when he had commissioned it from a photograph nearly sixty years earlier.

"You never stop feeling bad about it, nieto," he said. "But walking away from your feelings gets easier...if that makes sense."

Reuben nodded and then both men were looking at the painting.

"What do you think of you when you look at that painting, abuelo?"

It took a few moments for the older man to find his words.

"It's funny, I don't think you've ever asked about it before," he paused, when he spoke again his voice was quiet, reflective. "That picture has been there so long I don't see it anymore."

Hector got up with some difficulty and walked over to the painting, studying it as if he had never seen it before.

"Hearing your story I am reminded of why I had it made…"

The older man paused, remembering a time when *he* had been stricken by the death of someone under his care.

"The story about your patient, it reminds me of when I was starting out as a doctor…the last time I remember being saddened by one of my patients dying. I was younger than you, I want to say I was a few months from turning 28---"

"So, it was 1957."

"You always knew how old everyone in the family was," Hector laughed.

And Esmerelda always would scold the boy: "I do not need to be reminded how old I am, nieto."

Hector's smile faded but he forced it back on his face: Rueben was having a hard enough day without an old man's tears.

"A car and a truck came to the hospital where I worked," Hector began.

"There were injured people who had been wounded in a gunfight at a rancho a few hours to the west. All of the injured people were dead but one, a woman…"

2
(1957)

Hector was flirting with Esmerelda and she was flirting back. It was a good morning, the weather was fine and now his favorite nurse seemed amenable to possible getting coffee or some food or---

Shouting. Commotion near the entrance. Hector went towards the noise and Esmerelda followed. He didn't want her to; the yelling sounded like trouble. Two men in their forties, both dressed like hands on one of the ranchos, were carrying a woman into the hospital. The woman was unconscious so the men were struggling to hold her up and drag her into the hospital, her legs dragging behind her, the metal caps on the toes of her boots rasping and clicking against the tile. One of the older doctors started giving orders to Hector and Esmerelda and another young doctor who had also come running at the sound of commotion. The woman was a *gringa* but it had taken Hector a few seconds to realize that; her skin was dark as a Mexican's. The front of her shirt was so soaked with blood that drops of it were falling onto the tile.

"Is this the only one?" The head doctor asked the ranch hands.

"Yes," the one on the left of the gringa said. "The others died on the way here."

"Please bring her into this room and help us get her on the bed," the doctor said politely.

Hector was not surprised by how solicitous Dr. Hernandez was; the men clearly worked for someone important or at least dangerous if gunplay had been involved. The ranch hands helped the young doctors lay the gringa on a bed and then the one who had spoken before turned to Dr. Hernandez.

"We will leave now, Doctor," he nodded. "Don Miguel will know how kind and helpful you have been with Annie."

3
(1957)

The prognosis was grim for the gringa named Annie: Blood vessels had been irreparably damaged and the intestines perforated causing peritonitis.

"She may have hours, she may have days," Dr. Hendandez said to Hector after they closed her up. "Give her morphine to keep her comfortable but not too much; you tend to give them too much when they are suffering."

Hector had nodded, the dutiful apprentice doctor...inside he was fascinated by the patient: What was a gringa, and one in her fifties, doing as a soldier on a rancho? What was her story? He was so distracted that he did not even flirt with Esmerelda when instructing her about the morphine; the gringa filled his thoughts as he went through his rounds that morning and into the afternoon.

Annie was awake when Hector checked on her near the end of his shift. He wanted to ask her many questions but his English had been poor in those days.

She probably speaks our language, he realized. It made sense; the gringa was clearly respected by the men she worked with---that respect probably took many years to earn on the rancho.

"How are you feeling?" Hector asked in Spanish.

"Like I got shot in the guts," Annie smiled weakly.

Her Spanish was unaccented, as good as any Mexican's. The gringa winced when she shifted to make herself comfortable.

"Can I get you anything?" Hector asked. "Water?"

"Could I get more pain medicine?"

"I am sorry, we could not risk it."

She smiled at him wryly. The smile said: *Like dying would be worse than this pain.*

"You look like you have a lot of questions," Annie said. "Why don't you pour me a glass of water and sit yourself in that chair over there."

He wanted to protest, felt he should have been telling her to save her strength, but the gringa was correct: He *did* have a lot of questions. The young doctor left the room and went to fill a pitcher with water. Esmerelda watched him and was surprised that, again, he did not flirt with her.

"You look excited," the nurse said. "Like a boy."

"Annie is going to tell me her story."

"Annie?"

"The gringa that was shot."

"Do you think she would mind if I listened, as well?"

"I cannot imagine why she would mind."

Esmerelda took the pitcher from him and their fingers met, the first time their skin had touched. They looked at each other, forgetting Annie for a moment but only a moment. The nurse looked down shyly and then carried the water into the room where the gringa was staring at the ceiling as if looking for imperfections in the paint.

"I hope you do not mind if Esmerelda listens, as well," Hector said deferentially.

Annie shook her head.

"What is your name, doctor?" The patient asked.

"Hector. And this is Esmerelda."

"Hector," The patient laughed and then winced at the pain the laughter caused. "It is really a funny world. We were in a fight with a fellow named Hector and his men."

Emerelda helped Annie sit up, stacking pillows behind her and then bringing the cup of water to the patient's lips. The gringa smiled and thanked the nurse before continuing.

"I meant no disrespect to Don Hector--everything that happened was between you Mexicans; I just got in the middle of it, I guess."

She looked over at the glass and Esmerelda gave her more water. After taking a couple of sips, the patient continued.

"Don Miguel has always been good to me, he's been a good *jefe*, never seemed to hold it against me I am not a Mexican. When Don Hector and his men came up the road clearly meaning to shoot their guns I grabbed my pistol and took my place with Don Miguel and the fellows I've been working with for a few years now. There was no time to think about it or be scared; the whole thing happened naturally and fast---it only felt like a few seconds between grabbing my pistol and being shot."

Annie was being stoic but both the doctor and nurse could see the pain on her face, it was also revealed by the sweat on her brow and the way her fingers were clenching and unclenching. Hector could smell her bowel and had the feeling if they pulled the cover back her gown would be soaked in blood.

"There was time after the bullet punched me that I knew I had been shot but it didn't hurt, not right away," the patient continued. "I felt the punch of that bullet but I was caught up in fighting off Don Hector's men and it took a couple of minutes before the pain hit me."

She paused, now Hector could smell blood.

I should stop her---should.

"I looked down, saw the blood, and understood that the fellow across the courtyard had murdered me."

A wave of intense pain, the patient closed her eyes and cried out helplessly. Esmerelda gave Hector a dirty look.

"Please, you need to rest," the young doctor said. "Nurse, could you please make sure the wound is not bleeding too much."

Annie wasn't listening, her gaze was glassy.

"He has murdered you," she said so soft it seemed to herself. "You just haven't closed your eyes yet."

Hector and Esmerelda's shift ended at the same time. He wanted to drive her home but she said that it would anger her brothers. Sure enough, two angry young men who looked like Esmerela were waiting outside the hospital in a twenty year old Chevy sedan.

"I would like to ask you on a date," Hector said. "Would I need to speak to your brothers first?"

"It would be a good idea," Esmerelda agreed. "But this is not a good time: My younger sister was jilted by her man and this put my brothers in a vengeful mood."

"*Comprende*. Well, good night, Esmerelda."

She nodded and started walking towards the old Chevy which started when she approached. Esmerelda stopped halfway to the car and turned back to the doctor.

"I hope Annie will be up to telling more of her story tomorrow," she smiled.

"Me too."

The nurse nodded and turned around to continue to the back door behind the driver. The man behind the wheel hard stared Hector, nodded, and then turned to his sister with a fond smile and greeting as she climbed in.

4
(1957)

The next morning Hector and Esmerelda managed to sneak off to Annie's
room. There were six beds in the room, but the only other patient was a very
old man who mostly slept. The gringa appeared to be dealing with less pain
and seemed pleased to tell her story.

"Been working for Don Miguel maybe nine years now. He was as doubtful as
you at first: Not just a *norteamericano* but a woman to boot---a woman
around fifty."

Annie accepted the water cup, taking it from Esmerelda. Her hand was shaky
but when the nurse tried to help the patient waved her off.

"Sorry, but I ain't too good with people fussing over me," the older woman
said.

She shook a little water onto the covers but got a couple of sips before
holding the cup out for the nurse to take.

"I had those strikes against me," the patient continued, "but I had solid
references and when Don Miguel took me out to see if I could see if I could
shoot things off his fence I guess I did well. I never asked what Don Miguel
did for money, there seemed to be more to the ranch than just cattle, but it
never seemed my business. You see things after a few years but I chose to
ignore those things. Maybe ignoring things led to that fella across the
courtyard murdering me but I guess I am at peace with that."

"What brought you to Mexico?" Esmerelda asked.

"I came to Mexico looking for something that you could no longer find
where I am from. Those stories about cowboys and hired guns and shootouts
on dusty streets, good men and bad men...those stories have been an
obsession since I was a youngun."

She tried to sit up more but the movement delivered her a barrel of pain, you could tell by the way the patient screwed up her face.

"Maybe you should rest," Hector suggested.

"No. It's gonna hurt no matter what. At least going over the past is kind of a distraction."

The patient composed herself and continued.

"Even in New Mexico, which was still a territory when I was a child, what you see in Western movies these days was a thing of the past. When I was a kid people were getting telephones and motor cars; the past I was so fascinated with was slipping away---our town had a history of shootouts between bad men and good men but it wasn't talked about."

"Why not?" Hector asked.

Annie smiled slyly.

"The bad men had gone on and became the businessmen who you worked for and we all know what happens when you tell stories about the boss. This was why it was so hard for me to get the people I knew in my hometown to talk to me about the past, all the gunfights between bad men and good men-- that was until an older man took a room in the boarding house my mother ran. His name was Joseph, but everyone called him the Cavalier."

5
(1916)

The older man talking to her mother was like no one Annie had ever come across in her sixteen years: Old fashioned hat with a half eaten feather. Dingy blue cape. Knee high leather boots flared at the top. Mother looked doubtful but you could tell even through the window the stranger was a smooth talker, greasing his way into Mother's confidence enough to get one of the rooms that faced the street. For some reason Mother considered those the best rooms even if the ones in the back were quieter. The boarder had to be sixty with his faded blue cape and a mustache that curled up on the ends; you'd think that a man who could pay for mustache wax wouldn't have such shabby clothes and bags but Annie was starting to understand that people rarely made sense.

Days passed. It was clear to the young woman that her mother didn't like the new boarder but he had paid for a month in cash money and Mother had a soft spot for cash money. The boarder's name was Joseph but Mother and the other boarders called him the Cavalier and joshed about his attire and mannerisms. It seemed hypocritical to Annie, Mother acting superior to the new boarder, when you considered the shabby condition of the house and the poor meals that were served. Boarders would complain about Mother's food all the time. Annie agreed it wasn't fit even for a dog you wanted to poison but wasn't about to volunteer for the job; she had no interest in cooking or sewing or wearing dresses or any of that stuff girls her age were supposed to be doing. The teenager even wore pants---she would have worn a gun but there was no way Sheriff Barnes would have allowed it; New Mexico had been a state for four years and was trying mighty hard to at least pretend to be civilized.

The new boarder fascinated Annie: Joseph did not look like a gunfighter, he looked more like one of the Three Musketeers with his threadbare blue cape trimmed in what had been white. The trim had darkened and become shabby, just like the house he had taken a room in. Joseph looked old but not feeble old even if his mustache was white and his skin deeply sun lined. His accent sounded fake, almost English or something. To Annie he seemed like a character, maybe a flim-flam man. When she passed him in the hall or the dining room the boarder smelled like talcum powder, a little sweat, and some cologne she had never smelled before. To her it smelled expensive which seemed odd: Why was he spending money on mustache wax and cologne when his clothes were so worn.

"Annie, please run to the store and get Three some mustache wax."
Three, Mother was so unimpressed with the boarder he was not Mr So and So or Joseph, he was just a room number.
"What kind is he partial to?" The girl asked.
"Just get Dapper Dan or whatever," Mother said, handing over a quarter.
Annie got the wax and took it up to Room Three. Mother hadn't been worried about a young girl knocking on a strange man's door; she probably saw the Cavalier as a harmless old man, peculiar but not the sort to make unseemly advances. Joseph seemed winded when he answered the door with a kind smile that seemed genuine.
"Thank you," he looked her over but not in a lecherous way. "Well, I am guessing that you may not appreciate me calling you *miss*."
She had no idea what he meant and took offense. Joseph shook his head and smiled in such a charming fashion her anger broke up and drifted away.
"I meant no offense," he continued. "Why are you wearing an empty holster, if I may ask?"

"Sheriff doesn't allow guns within town limits, sir."

"Can you shoot a pistol?"

That felt good; him talking to her like a person and not some strange girl who preferred hunting over cooking.

"Yes, sir," she smiled proudly. "Been shooting a few years now."

The new guest looked around and then winked at Annie.

"Oh, then we had best keep one of my possessions our little secret."

He walked over to a chair where a carpet bag made of a faded red floral corduroy sat. The old man dug around a bit and pulled out an old pistol. The way Joseph handled it the girl could tell he was no shootist, the cautious shapes his hands made as he cradled it.

"A Colt Jim Fisk," she said with open awe."I haven't seen many of those."

He nodded and handed it over to her. It wasn't loaded. Even though it was clear that Joseph was no shootist, that pistol told her that the man in the cape had lived through some adventures in the past. The revolver was pristine, no nicks or scratches; it had probably never been in a holster or dropped in the dirt or anything like that.

"As you can tell I am not a hired gun or anything of that nature," the boarder said. "Everyone carried a pistol back then..."

Joseph sat on the bed and the smile changed, becoming sad. No, not just sad, *wistful.*

"I don't know why I haven't sold it, no one carries a gun these days."

"Out at the mines they do, sir," Annie offered "I see them checking their guns in at the Sheriff's office."

He was studying her and she was studying him. Annie *knew* the old fellow had to have a lot of stories about a time she wished she had lived through. Joseph seemed both lonely and in need of an audience, it probably wouldn't be hard to coax interesting stories out of him.

"I need to get settled in now," he said. "I do appreciate your running to the store for me--what is your name?"

"Anna or Annie."

"You don't like that name, I can see that."

"I prefer A.R. but I would appreciate it if you didn't say that around Momma."

"Understood. Your mother would probably prefer you calling me Mr. Gellis, but between you and I Joseph is fine."

"Yes, sir. Joseph."

Taking her leave of the new boarder, Annie went downstairs to where Mother was speaking with one of the long term borders, a fat man with a large mustache. He smiled in the girl's direction but she could see the smile was as fake as the hair on his head. Weeks later the boarder would be found out to be a pervert who was eventually run out of town for peeping on girls Annie's age and younger.

"And what do you think of the Cavalier, Miss Anna?"

Fat Pervert licked his lips after asking his question.

"That's a queer name," A.R. replied.

"It was because of the cape, I believe," the boarder continued after allowing his eyes to drift over her body. "I remember seeing him around when I was a boy."

That seemed unlikely as Fat Pervert appeared the same age as Joseph. Even though she didn't care for the man Annie was hungry for any information he may have had on the newest boarder.

"What is his story?" She asked.

Fat Pervert looked her up and down again without a care with regards to the girl's mannish attire or that Mother was close enough to swat him.

"He was a character, sold patent medicines from a wagon, was what they would call a confidence man."

Mother held her hands up to silence Fat Pervert.

"That is enough. Mr. Gellis may have done some questionable things in the past, but he is elderly now and surely retired. Can't we talk about something else?"

And that was it, the door was closed; Annie understood she would have to get any information on Joseph from somewhere else. She asked their pardons and walked off. Fat Pervert's eyes followed her hoping for a hint of something he had allowed to curse him.

6
(1916)

It was March when Joseph moved into the room that overlooked the street and flowers were starting to bloom. Over breakfast or supper the boarders would talk about the war that had been going on in Europe for nearly two years. They called it the *Great War*, great as in *terrible*, like no war in the past. It was nothing to A.R. and she never joined in their conversations...not they never tried to include her. It was plain to her that they saw her as a strange girl who preferred dressing like a boy right down to the empty holster. The boarders treated Joseph even worse, bowing to him as a joke and pretending to treat him like royalty or something. Maybe he made his own mess by wearing that cape, but Annie understood the need to be in your own mess and would sit with him after serving the guests.

After a couple weeks the old man and the girl were comfortable around each other. They'd stroll around town and Annie had no doubt people were whispering about them.

"It is good that this town has moved on," Joseph said during one of their walks. "Those days, they were brutish, A.R., nothing to romanticize."

"I can tell you miss them, though," she replied. *And I wish I could have lived them.*

Forty years later, at the end of her life, Annie could still recall the smallest details from her walks with the man they called the Cavalier. The two of them would invariably stop under an apple tree, and even lying in a Mexican hospital bed she could recall the smell of the fruit and everything Joseph had said.

"I miss being young, A.R. I miss having adventures," the old man had said. "The time when I was young enough to have them, though, it was a hard time."

Annie said nothing in response, waiting eagerly for the boarder to continue. Most times he would smile and speak in the manner of a man with much life still inside him. His clothes were worn and he had little money but he was always "days away" from "something working out grandly." He never revealed to her what that may have been and Annie never saw any change in his status or purse; some things he kept a secret but it was clear his untold plans had not come to fruition.

I had a dream about death last night.

That was the first time Joseph showed Annie his vulnerable side. He hadn't been down to breakfast. In fact, it was early in the afternoon and she hadn't seen him around the house. When his door was knocked on Joseph sighed for her to enter if she wanted so A.R. turned the knob and walked in. He was sitting on his bed looking sad. It was queer to see the boarder just sitting on the bed all sad, distinctly out of character.

"I had a dream about death last night," he said, his voice raspy. "It's probably because we've been talking about the past so much."

He motioned for her to sit in the chair next to the window. A strong light was coming through the lace curtains and they could hear two boarders arguing about whether or not the Kaiser was in the wrong. Joseph stood and made a fuss over his cravat but it was clear he just needed something to do with his hands.

"My dream was about two friends," he started. "Two young men, boys really, not much older than you, A.R. You know friends...as close as they are there is always a piece of grit in there, a quarrel. One night these boys got to drinking and, fed by liquor, the quarrel grew to a monster. This was before the law

20

about checking your guns. In the middle of the fussing the pistols came out and one of the boys was shot down, wounded badly...already dying and howling in pain as he lay in the street. The other instantly sobered and, seeing that he had killed his friend, started sobbing."

Joseph's voice had grown quieter and quieter; by the last few words she could barely hear him. There was nothing you could say to such a terrible story--- Annie could see it, two boys dressed like cowboys, one holding a gun with tears running down his face and the other twisting in slow motion as he lay on the street.

"It wasn't like those books you've read, A.R. I believe most of those were written by people who had never been to a town like this. If they had ever seen something like those two friends jerking their pistols..."

Annie could see him catching himself, forcing his usual carefree nature back into place. He stood at full height and smiled over at her; he did that, but his eyes hadn't changed, they were still full of pain.

"Ah, we don't need any of that old misery, do we? Help me with my cape, I believe today is too beautiful not to get a walk in!"

Joseph was putting up such an effort with his disguise that she felt obligated to play along. He had passed a curse to her, though; to the end of her days Annie would dream of those two friends from time to time.

7
(1957)

"Can we give her more morphine?" Esmerelda asked Hector in the hallway. "Her pain, it is very bad."

He liked her standing close, could smell the soap she used and the food she ate; all the scents that had embedded in her uniform.

"I will speak to Dr. Hernandez---"

"You are a doctor, you can make this decision."

What she said seemed harsh but looking at her face Hector could see that she meant it playfully.

"I am a doctor, and I would like to remain one," he said with a smile. "I will go look in on her. Will you come?"

"Sadly, I have a boss, as well," Esmerelda replied.

"Are you brothers still in a bad mood?"

Her smile changed, became shy. Esmerelda looked down at the floor for a couple of seconds before being able to face the doctor.

"Ask me in four days," she said.

Annie was on her side, curled up and wheezing.

"That position," Hector said softly. "It may be making the pain worse."

"This is hellfire," the patient wheezed. "It feels like my innards are on fire."

He couldn't stand to see his patient suffer. Hector went to the cabinet on the side of the room, prepared a light syringe of morphine, and administered it to Annie. The doctor sat in the chair, as anxious as his patient for the drug to take effect. After a few minutes, Annie relaxed and some of the pain left her face.

"How long do I have, doctor?" She asked, her voice rough and barely a whisper.

"We don't know. Honestly, I am surprised you are still with us."

Was that the wrong thing to say? Too honest? The patient didn't seem bothered by his words.

"I had a dream about death last night," she was thinking in English, maybe because she had been talking about the old days, and it took some work to put her thoughts into Spanish.

"Where I was...it was a dark and lonely place. Peace, deep solitude. When I awoke I couldn't move; there was a panic that I was pinned in by the walls of a coffin...this room was dark as a grave must be. It took all sorts of effort to sit up. The pain was awful but the pain was good---I was still alive."

She looked over at the pitcher of water. The doctor poured a glass and she allowed him to pour it past her lips. After a few seconds she nodded and Hector took the glass away.

"The dream changed," Annie continued. "I went back to the day Don Hector and his men drove up. That morning as I was getting ready I had seen myself differently in the mirror: An old face was staring back, a stranger's face or maybe just a person I wasn't ready to be. It was like looking in that mirror and seeing a killer standing behind me, smiling as he prepared to open my throat with a knife."

She trailed off and stared at the ceiling. The patient was so still and quiet the doctor wondered for a moment if she had passed.

"Death always smiles at you when he does his deed," Annie continued. "I brushed him away just as Joseph did on a regular basis. He had the aches and pains of someone getting old but he ignored them or tried to. I recall him spending a lot of time trimming his mustache. It must have been dashing when he was younger; when I knew Joseph it was mostly white."

The patient looked over at Hector. She was dying, he could see that. No, she had always been dying, but the dying process had sped up that morning.

"I moved away from the mirror to be younger again," Annie continued. "A car pulled up to the house and I heard men shouting that Don Hector was on his coming up the road in a sedan and a flatbed with men in the back...I got treated differently by Don Miguel, maybe it was because I was older than his other hands---"

She saw something in Hector's face and her expression switched to offended for a couple of seconds then amused.

"Are you thinkin' Don Miguel was partial to me because I am a woman? I doubt that; there were never any flirtations between my boss and I. He enjoyed asking me about the United States and liked speaking English with me, none of the others could speak English. Don Miguel and I would drink mescal and talk late. This is one reason I didn't hesitate to grab my pistol when Don Hector and his men drove up to the house."

Another nod towards the cup, another few sips.

"I woke up last night trying to remember why Joseph and I went down to Mexico---what had led to it? No, I woke up because of the pain and was trying to occupy my mind. I thought and thought and eventually saw the dining room of the boarding house. Two men were eating and talking about the war in Europe.

The war to end all wars, that's what they called it then. It wasn't going well and many lives had been lost. One man said he hoped that the United States wouldn't be dragged in. The other countered that he hoped the U.S.A. stepped in to teach the Huns a lesson. I was standing nearby, about to ask if they wanted more food."

8
(1916)

Joseph walked in and they stopped talking to stare at him. They smiled but there was a meanness in their eyes. Maybe in his old-fashioned clothes and cloak he reminded them of the past; the town was trying to pretend the past hadn't happened because the past was full of violence and the corruption had been out in the open; the wretched beginnings of men who would later pass for being reputable. Annie was angry that those fellows in her shabby boarding house thought they were better than Joseph---how could they be so arrogant? The way they carried on you'd think they were one deal or business concern away from being up there with the wealthy men who ran the town.

"Good morning, gentlemen," The man in the cape said in a strong voice.

"Mornin', Joseph."

Mother walked in with her smells of flowers and sweat. Annie had overheard those same men laughing about the way mother smelled.

"Late once again, Joesph," Mother scolded. "I see why they called you *The Cavalier*; you sure are cavalier about showing up for breakfast on time."

"My apologies, Mrs. Crabbe."

"Why did they call you the Cavalier?" That question from the man who wanted the US into the war, egg literally on his face.

"The cloak, I guess. It's an old name from another time."

"Joseph here was a character back in the day," another boarder snorted. "And with his advancing years it would seem he hasn't lost that quality."

The men at the table laughed at that one and Joseph tried to join in. He *did* feel old; had told Annie that he had been feeling out of sorts. Climbing stairs left him gasping for breath. He was about to turn sixty but despite that had never felt *old* before and didn't like it, didn't like it at all---Joseph said as much to the girl.

After eating Joseph went back up to his room. He was feeling small; he'd never admit such a thing but Annie had learned to read him. She would try to imagine what he was like alone behind the closed door of Room Three. Forty years later in a Mexican hospital she would understand all too well, looking around at where your life had ended up: A room. Maybe forty dollars to your name. All your belongings fitting in a battered suitcase and a carpet bag coming apart at the seams. A revolver. The girl imagined him pulling out his Jim Fisk and turning it over in his hands. The Cavalier was no shootist but there had probably been a few times in his life when he had shot that pistol.

A couple of hours later he came down to the kitchen where Annie was doing chores. There was a smile on his face but his eyes still looked sad. Joseph agreed with her suggestion to take their daily walk. Normally he put on a big show, smiling and talking in a theatrical way, but not that afternoon.

"The world is in too big a hurry for its own good."

He said that so softly it almost sounded as if he were talking to himself.

"Ten years ago," he continued as they paused beneath the apple tree, "seeing a motorcar was a rare occurrence; now it seems like everybody has one. I hoped it was just a fad."

"Joseph?"

A familiar voice: English with a Mexican accent belonging to a *Mexicano* with a big belly and gray hair who was walking towards them.

"Pepe! *Como esta?*" Joseph was laughing, seeming like his old self. "My word, this is a very old friend of mine, A.R."

The men shook hands excitedly and then Joseph introduced the girl.

"What have you been doing, Senor Joe?" Pepe asked.

Nothing, my friend, nothing. That was probably what he was thinking.

26

"Oh, I have a couple of deals I've been planning out. How about you? Still working for Harmon?"

"Yes. I run his ranches on both sides of the border. Imagine that---Harmon trusting a Mexican."

"His faith is not misplaced, *mi amigo*, not at all."

Pepe's jovial face clouded.

"I have some bad news, I'm afraid."

"What's that?" Joseph asked

"*El Hombre*, he is dead."

The easy joy left Joseph's face, he looked tired and old again.

"Really?" He asked softly. "How is that even possible?"

"I saw his gun belt; I do not think he would be without it if he were alive."

"Did you find it somewhere?"

Pepe looked uncomfortable---Annie wondered if it was the story he was telling or if he felt sorry for Joseph who was acting weak and old.

"No. An Apache came in to trade it a few months back."

"An *Apache*? I didn't know any of them were left."

"Most are gone but there are still a few and they are still trouble."

"Did he know who killed our friend?"

"He would not say. Maybe they ambushed him, caught him off guard. I guess he was old; he was old even when he saved us."

When he saved us? Annie's ears pricked up but she worked to keep her face casual.

I was right about that Jim Fisk, it had been used in some sort of gunfight, she thought to herself.

"He was in his forties back then which would make him in his seventies now, if he were alive," Joseph said thoughtfully.

"Maybe. This Apache, he said el Hombre was left where he died and his bones are still out there."

27

Joseph made a face. Later he would tell A.R. that it was disquieting to imagine someone he had known as nothing more than scattered bones.

"I am sorry, Senor Joe," Pepe said, "but I need to get going. I have to pick up some supplies---"

"Yes," Joseph smiled, working to be as cavalier as his nickname. "I have an appointment I am due at, myself. Good seeing you, Pepe."

"Yes, you too, Senor Joe, A.R."

Joseph strutted off on his way to an imaginary appointment with Annie in tow. When his old friend was out of sight he stopped and stared down at the wooden sidewalk.

"Pepe seems to be doing well, seems to be set for the rest of his life..."

But what will become of me? He didn't say that but it was on his face. Sure, he had experienced many adventures in his life, a lot of *fun*, but what security did he have? His sadness was replaced by an emotion she hadn't seen on his face before: Anxiety.

"You alright, Joseph?"

"I have this pain in my chest. If I sit down I'm sure it will pass."

I am not going to let this nonsense get me down.

Maybe he wanted to say that but was too overcome to even whisper it.

"You don't look too well," Annie said. "We need to get you to the doctor."

Joseph was too weak to stand or even answer so she waved a passing buggy down.

"My friend here is having a bad spell, can you help me get him to the doctor?"

"A spell?" The man looked confused. He had a red simple face---probably a laborer at one of the big houses on the edge of town.

"His heart," Annie said. "I think something is going wrong with it."

The man on the buggy grunted in understanding and climbed down. He was rough and clumsy as he helped Joseph into the back. The older man muttered something into the girl's ear and then closed his eyes. The man driving the buggy cracked the reins and looked in the back of his wagon.

"What did he say?"

"I think he said 'I am not going to let this nonsense get me down'."

9
(1957)

An orderly took inventory of the morphine in the cabinet. Dr. Hernandez read the inventory and asked his subordinates to explain the missing doses. Hector quickly confessed and Dr. Hernandez took him aside.

"Why did you not consult me?" The older doctor asked harshly. "You are one of my most promising staff, why would you risk your job here?"

"She was in a lot of pain, Dr. Hernandez. I couldn't stand seeing her suffer." The older man's expression softened.

"We've all been in your place, doctor," Dr. Hernandez said softly. "None of us want to see our patients in a place of misery, but you must not risk giving your patient too much morphine...unless the two of you have an understanding."

It took a few moments for Hector to understand: *An understanding;* an agreement to set the patient free of this world of pain.

"I am not a Mexican and I never will be," Annie said out of the blue as Hector was checking her pulse. "Even after all my years down here I am still on the stoop, not knocking just waiting for a soul to open the door to me. Everyone is friendly, most people are good to me, but I came from somewhere else and no one has forgotten that---especially me."

"You must like it down here," Hector said. "To stay so long."

"The winters are mild here aside from the nights when the cold becomes mean. The winter that just ended...some nights I would ache. I am not that sixteen year old who could wander off into the hills and sleep rough for days. I am not even the 22 year old who crossed the border and has rarely gone back over it."

She paused, shrugged towards the glass of water, and the doctor helped her take a drink.

"Maybe my memories of the man known as the Cavalier are so clear to me because I too have been feeling time running down. I knew I was done for when Dr. Hernandez touched my arm and smiled at me kindly. He had been all business and none too kind---the only thing that could explain his change of heart is that I am done for."

Annie paused, looked up at the ceiling, and was still and quiet for nearly a minute.

"The pain is moving further away, maybe into the past. I am not sure I will get to the end of this story, but I will give it my all. Don't concern yourself that this is troubling me. No, if anything it is taking my mind off my troubles."

10
(1916)

Joseph had never been in a hospital before as a patient. Visits to them had always made him ill-at-ease: The medicinal smells. The grunts and groans of the infirm. The feeling of solemnness. Now, he was a guest in one and too weak to leave. He was alert but too feeble to do more than weakly say he was "alright" when it was clear that he wasn't. They had put him in a ward with eight other men. The ceilings were high and the walls appeared to have been recently white-washed much as they appear to be here.

Blood, he thought morbidly, *someone probably bled all over them.*

Another terrible thought---what was happening to his mind? Why was he having so many bleak thoughts and dreams? Joseph had always prided himself on his upbeat nature and now there was all this darkness on the edges creeping in. A doctor entered the ward with a smile on his face and crossed the room to his new patient.

"I am Doctor Slane, do you know your name?" He was a soft looking, clean-shaven man maybe in his mid-thirties.

"Joseph."

Doctor Slane nodded pleasantly and pulled a chair over to the bed. He probably thought his patient was too stricken to remember his last name; Annie had the feeling Joseph would be fine with that assumption. She listened as the doctor asked a series of questions about the attack which the man on the bed struggled to answer and A.R. tried to fill in the blanks when Joseph didn't have an answer. Slane listened and at the end of the questioning looked unsure in a way no one wants their doctor to look.

"I think you had a heart attack," he said.

The confusion on Joseph's face made him look old and pitiful.

"I have never heard of such a thing," he said weakly.

"Until a few months ago neither had I," the doctor replied with a gentle smile. The old man experienced another wave of faintness but mercifully most of the pain had left his chest or at least that's what Joseph told Annie when she asked. The doctor was watching his patient carefully; he looked concerned and the concern on his face made A.R. and Joseph even more anxious.

"Am I going to die?" The patient asked.

The doctor's smile thinned but the gentleness remained in his eyes.

"Yes, but I don't think it will be today or tomorrow for that matter. You just need to lead a quiet life from now on."

Joseph did not respond with words but his eyes said everything; forty years later Annie would recall how eyes looked and finally understand what was going on behind them: The patients remembered how they had been decades earlier, darker haired and laughing while leaping off low, stone walls or horses...then the memory of joy and strength turns into a view of a shabby room.

"Sadly, things have been going that way for some time," Joseph said glumly.

It was obvious that the doctor had no idea how to respond---who was this odd, older man in the shabby cape? The town was still small enough for rumors and stories to travel easily.

He must be the one they call the Cavalier.

"Has your heart been under any stress?" Slane asked after a few moments had passed.

Joseph didn't want to be the one to drag the darkness in from the edges. He liked life free of burdens and troubles and was trying to push back at shadows that, in the end, had grown too strong.

"My heart has been heavy, if that matters," he sighed.

The doctor's right hand moved towards the bed, maybe to rest reassuringly on Joseph's arm, only to be pulled back before making contact. The doctor's expression remained kind; it seemed real and deep and when he spoke his voice had cracks on the surface.

"Well, all I can suggest is to find a way to lift that weight. We'll keep you overnight and release you in the morning."

Doctor Slane rose from the chair and put it back exactly where it had been. Joseph watched him go to the other beds with the same gentle smile and tone of voice. The patient closed his eyes tight and struggled to find a place in his mind to escape to.

Four days passed before Joseph was allowed to return to the room overlooking the street. Each time Annie checked on her friend he was sitting on the edge of the bed. Joseph put on a brave show each time, getting up with a big smile and happy words: *I am not going to let this nonsense get me down.* It was clear even then it was just a show but each time A.R. smiled and went along because, even at sixteen, she understood that was what friends did. The troubles remained in his eyes---what was he thinking? Maybe he was preoccupied with the hospital ward and the thought of bones bleaching out in the desert. Even though his strength was returning he was probably shaken by his own mortality slapping him in the face then kicking him to the ground. Lying in that iron framed bed in that room that smelled of medicine, Joseph understood that it wouldn't be the last time in a hospital---he was getting older; as much as he wanted to deny it, he was getting old in a world he no longer recognized: Motorcars. Telephones. A terrible war in Europe unlike any other in human existence. What had happened to the world he knew? What had happened to the strength that had made any problems seem trivial? What had happened to the innocent times?

"How are you feeling?" Annie would ask at the beginning of each visit.

"Much better, thank you," Joseph would always reply with a smile.

Those were the things they said to each other, polite conversation in a place that made both uneasy and stole their ability to make words.

This getting old business is for the birds, I'll tell you. I never was a morbid sort but now I find myself thinking about death.

Annie thought that on the fourth day of her own hospital stay, words Joseph had said quietly forty-one years earlier; one of the rare times Joseph opened up to her.

"I think it's good to think about death," A.R. said. "It helps you appreciate life more."

She felt proud having come up with that, it seemed like a mature thing to say.

"Maybe," Joseph, putting up an agreeable smile but still looking weak.

"Who was the friend you were talking to before your heart attack?" A.R. asked.

"Pepe: We used to travel together many years ago."

Annie thought of the Jim Fisk and got excited; maybe talking about Pepe would bring up more stories about the old days. She was greedy for those stories and felt guilty for being alright with depleting her friend's rest.

"It sounded like he was talking about someone you knew who died," Annie prompted, guilt or no guilt.

It was a while before Joseph spoke. An old fellow three beds over moaned and then there was the smell of shit. Annie's friend winced; he clearly smelled it too.

"I knew him by reputation," Joseph explained quietly, "he was a shootist."

"A hired gun?"

That question seemed to amuse the old man.

"Oh, no one hired the Stoic; he had no use for money."

Annie was excited; a story was coming. She sat forward in the chair and then sat back so as not to give away her eagerness.

"*The Stoic?* That's quite a name."

35

A lot of weariness left Joseph's face, he was probably remembering the old days.

"He was quite a legend back then, a very mysterious man. Very skilled with a gun, saved the lives of myself and three others."

"What happened?"

"We were a problem to the people who run this town. They brought in several hired guns to kill us. Only reason it didn't happen was the Stoic."

Joseph rubbed his hands together slowly and his smile disappeared.

"I've been thinking of his bones just lying out there in the desert; it doesn't seem right...a man like that deserves the respect of a decent burial."

"You *did* say that he saved your life."

The nearby moaner made a terrible sound again. Joseph closed his eyes again, maybe to force away his awareness of the other patient. When he reopened his eyes, he stared at the far wall.

"He did. The problem is that his bones are in Mexico and I am sure you have read of the violence down there."

"Yes."

"This afternoon I got the idea to find his bones and bring them back to New Mexico, but it is a foolish idea."

He looked genuinely sad.

"And I am a foolish, old man," Joseph added.

Anne sat forward in the chair and took the hand closest to her in both of hers. It felt cold, that worried her.

"It isn't foolish to want to do right by your friends. What about the others he saved? Maybe they would want to help you. I know I would."

Joseph glanced at her with a smile then went back to staring at the far wall.

"Pepe probably would, he's as loyal as an old dog. The others? I don't know, we parted ways not long after what happened in Deming. The last I saw any of them was in Los Huesos."

"The bones," Annie said thoughtfully.

"Pardon?"

"Los Huesos, the bones."

"Yes, and it was the perfect name for that grim little town."

Something about the story was making her friend ill at ease so A.R. changed tack.

"You never really explain to me why they call you the Cavalier."

"It's a nick-name," Joseph sighed. "An old one, one I outgrew many years ago but no one will allow me to live down. I was cavalier back then, not a care in the world, nothing could stop me."

His voice began to break up on the last two works. He composed himself and continued.

"Like I said, I outgrew that name many years ago."

Those words are ghosts in that room but Annie needed to know what he meant.

"I am not a young man anymore," he said in a heavier tone of voice. "I can't sleep out in the open and ride for days or run across fields like I used to. This heart attack closed the door."

A heart attack, a rifle shot from across a courtyard decades later; everything vibrant and possible in one moment and dark the next.

"So, you're just going to give up?" The girl asked.

A.R. was trying to goad him because she needed him to be *himself*, the Cavalier. The young woman wanted to lock Joseph in a closet so the Cavalier could be free. Anger flashed across his face, he was angry at her but at least the life in him had sparked.

"I don't know...this has been a strange couple of days," he said briskly. "I have been having thoughts that are very new to me. Maybe they will become less troubling with time, but right now there is a peculiar heaviness to my heart."

Forty years later it would be easy for Annie to recall his exact words he said because, in that Mexican hospital room, she was writing them under her skin.

The day Joseph was released with the hospital, Annie walked with him down to supper. The other boarders gawked at him, an odd man well on in years wearing a cape and riding boots. His clothes were clean and well cared for but frayed and decades out of style---*he* was out of style. The world had moved on but maybe he didn't need the world with it's motorcars and telephones and general state of impatience. He was *the Cavalier*, maybe the name suited him, maybe living up to that name was the only thing that could bring him true happiness. The smile on his face became more natural and he laughed aloud not caring what anyone else thought---
I am not going to let this nonsense get me down!

11
(1957)

After his shift, Hector would return to his *tio's* house where he had lived since leaving his parent's home more than a decade earlier; he would live with them until he married, that was how it was done. Their house was a good size with enough rooms that the young doctor had a small one of his own. His cousins had to share rooms with their *hermanos* or *hermanas*, which Hector felt guilt for, but Tio Armundo was adamant:

You need privacy for your studies. Soon, you will marry, maybe that Esmerelda you talk about, and then Juan will get your room.

The four days the gringa had been under his care and telling her stories Hector's thoughts had been going places they had never gone before: He had never been curious about the old days, for example, when men wore guns everywhere and there was barely any law. It was still that way out in the country---the shootout between Dons Hector and Miguel was proof of that---but in the city you rarely saw people wearing guns. Getting home that night, he found Abuelo Armundo sitting out front smoking his pipe and drinking a beer. His grandfather had to be seventy---clearly he would remember the old days. The old man was gruff with the others in the house, normally Hector was wary of his abuelo but that night he was curious enough to get past his fear.

"Buenos noches, abuelo," he smiled, dropping into the chair next to the older man.

Abuelo grunted, took a sip of his beer.

"You smell like the hospital," he said in a rough but quiet voice.

Hector ignored the observation; the old man *always* had this anger about him.

"I have an interesting patient, abuelo. A gringa, she was a soldier for a rancho out in the hills. She was shot and now she has been telling me stories about the old days."

Armundo grunted, lit his pipe, and got the smoke going.

"The old days were shit, *nieto*, good that they passed."

"Were they not exciting? Do you remember the Revolution?"

Instead of getting excited about talking about the old days (which Hector had hoped), his abuelo just looked more irritated.

"The Revolution was shit, a bunch of *pendejos* with guns shooting each other."

He took a sip of his beer, looked over at his grandson.

"Look at this house, nieto, your *tío* has put in plumbing; you grew up without a toilet in the house, is shitting out of doors anything to miss?"

His abuelo mentioning the place Hector had grown up brought up other memories for the younger man, bad ones. The older man saw the sadness on his face, grunted, and relit his pipe.

"You are free of the past, nieto, I am free of the past...let both of us be glad."

The next morning Annie was unconscious. The smells of blood and feces were stronger, her time had to be close. Hector was surprised when she opened her eyes and motioned for water. After he helped her drink from the cup, the old woman continued her story.

"It was after the second world war that I came to work for Senor Miguel," her voice was rougher, weaker. "I had worked at another hacienda for some years but the owner had died and his son had no use for a *gringa*. No, he had nothing for me but insults and I was too old to be a gal he kept around for appearances."

That took a lot out of her. Hector offered to leave so she could rest but Annie shook her head.

"Like I said, doctor, telling these stories is a good way to escape this agony in my gut. I can't get far from it, just far enough to get a little peace."

She struggled to sit up and the pain made her groan. Hector moved to help her but she waved him off. Esmerelda walked in and stood close to the doctor; he enjoyed feeling the warmth coming off her and smelling her smells.

"You two look good together," the patient said with a weak but warm smile before continuing.

"My friend Macho told me that Senor Miguel was looking for a hand that could shoot and keep the stock safe from varmints," Annie continued. "I had been in Mexico for twenty years and understood perfectly what he meant by that. Funny it would be Macho that would kill me in a courtyard but that is nothing I hold against him; it was out of loyalty to our employers that we drew on each other."

She motioned for the water, this time it was Esmerelda that helped her with the cup.

"The past couple of years it has become clear to me that my youth was long behind me," the patient continued. "The world I had been chasing since I was a young gal had long slipped in the past."

Her breathing had become more ragged, she paused to get her wind.

"When I came across the Cavalier I was young enough to believe that I could track that world down if I just kept going to wilder and more brutal places. The Apaches slinked across the border at the end of the last century. In your country I have spoken to folks that come across Apaches and that the Indians were as fierce as they had been back in the day. Of course, that was many years ago but I would like to think some of those Apaches are still out there, deep in the mountains, still wild and ready to send arrows rocketing into flesh. They were probably still raiding ranchos back when Joseph and I became friends."

12
(1916)

The Harmon ranch was a few miles south of town. Having sold his horse long ago, the Cavalier had no way of traveling to it. Annie walked with him to the edge of town and followed his stare down the road. He said nothing but she could tell by his face and posture that her friend was doubtful that he could walk all the way to that ranch.

"You worried you might have another heart attack?" She asked, immediately regretting her choice of words.

Joseph drew up his shoulders and became the Cavalier again; there was life in him again and it pleased her to see it.

"Better to die on the side of the road than in that damned rooming house, no offense," he doffed his hat to her and smiled charmingly.

A truck eased to a stop next to him. An old colored man was behind the wheel.

"You folks need a ride?" He asked.

"Are you going as far as the Harmon ranch?" Joseph inquired.

"I imagine I am, sir, seeing as I am the cook."

The Cavalier pulled himself into the cab and Annie jumped in the bed with the crates and sacks that had been neatly placed back there.

"Thank you for your kindness, I am Joseph and back there is A.R."

"Name is Abel, but people call me Chokes."

A cook named Chokes, this day is turning into a real peach, Annie thought.

"Pardon me, sir, but are you the one they call the Cavalier?"

A.R. could feel her friend tense up.

"I suppose," Joseph replied, "though it was never a kind nickname."

Chokes rested both of his dark hands on the peak of the steering wheel.

"Ah, I imagine folks are just jealous. People don't do anything around here, have no imagination."

The tension left Joseph and he laughed easily.

"I always had an imagination, that is for sure," he said.

Chickens had run out onto the dirt road. Chokes tooted the horn but the birds didn't scatter. He slowed to a slow walking speed and eased around the willful hens.

"They said you knew the Stoic back in the day," the driver said.

Joseph looked over with surprise.

"You heard of the Stoic?"

"Yes, sir. You can tell I've been around some days, I imagine, will be sixty-five in August. I remember back when this area was a lot wilder and everyone seemed to carry a gun."

"I remember those days as well, Chokes."

Past the birds, the old cook got back up to a good clip.

"The Stoic was a legend, may as well have *been* a legend as I never saw him myself, just heard stories. One involved you, as I said."

"Yes, he saved my life."

"Wonder what happened to him..."

The joy the man in the cape had been feeling dissipated; A.R. could feel it break up and drift off.

"From what I heard he passed away somewhere in Mexico," Joseph said softly. "A friend of mine came across his gunbelt and was told it was near some bones out in the desert."

Chokes looked troubled by that thought.

"What a shame, a fine man like that who saved a lot of folks just lying out there."

"I agree." Joseph stopped there; he didn't want to explain why he was on his way to the ranch and risk the cook spreading stories that could affect Pepe's reputation.

"Who are you going to see at the ranch?" The driver asked.

"Pepe Gonzales," Joseph said.

"We got three Pepe Gonzaleses."

"He's a foreman or maybe even a manager, maybe ten years younger than us; rotund fellow."

"I know him, he's a good man," Chokes looked at Joseph with a warm smile.

"That he is."

Chokes parked at the main house and had a boy fetch Pepe. He then had another boy get Joseph and Annie glasses of lemonade.

"You going to be alright, Mr. Joseph?"

"Yes, Abel, I genuinely appreciate your kindness."

"You're going to find him and do right by him," the cook smiled kindly.

"I will certainly try."

Pepe was walking up the road, he looked worried. Harmon probably knew of his past, everyone in the area did, but to see him talking to *the Cavalier* might not look good.

Nevertheless, Joseph explained to Annie later, *this is a matter of honor and honorable deeds, giving a respected man a proper burial. That makes it worth a little ding on a man's reputation.*

"Joseph---*como esta*?"

The man in a cape didn't bother with pleasantries.

"We need to bury him, Pepe," Joseph said firmly. "We need to do right by him."

It seemed the Mexican understood what he was saying and it also seemed that didn't like it.

"He is dead, Joseph," the Mexican said with his own firmness. "There is nothing we can do for him."

The man in the cape looked around at the ranch, the fine main house, barns, and fields of cattle.

"He deserves a proper Christian burial---he *saved* us. You remember what happened," Joseph said.

"Yes."

Pepe was a good man, he had probably already been feeling ill at ease at the thought of the Stoic's bones just scattered out there in the wastelands. But, he was also probably concerned about his standing with the Harmons---the situation would have to be handled carefully. Ruefully, the Mexican recalled that the Cavalier *knew* people, knew how to *work* them---this included his friends.

"I do not take your standing at this ranch lightly, Pepe. How about this: I will travel to Los Angeles and speak to the others; in the meantime I ask that you simply think about it---will you do that for me?"

Pepe looked around at the ranch. Annie guessed he was thinking about all the work he had done over the years to get to where he was, a trusted hand in a solid position, especially for a Mexican.

"Yes." And then Pepe looked worried and possibly confused. "Travel? You can't call or telegraph them?"

"No. This has to be done in person."

Pepe shrugged. Others were watching the old friends talk; the manager of the ranch was clearly uncomfortable about that and the Cavalier understood he had to wrap things up.

"I hate to do this, old friend, but I am a bit short on funds at the moment..."

Pepe winced.

"How much do you need?" He asked.

"I don't know, maybe fifty dollars. Anything I do not use on my travels I will promptly return."

"Give me a couple of days, I will have it brought to your rooming house."

I will have it brought to your rooming house. The subtext stung Joseph a bit but he kept it to himself.

"Splendid, I will be off then."

13
(1916)

Annie did not tell her mother that she was traveling with one of the boarders to Los Angeles. Effectively, she was running away from home and could only imagine that trouble that would be waiting when she got back. The Cavalier believed that his young friend had gotten permission and A.R. never made an effort to alter his beliefs. The trip was uneventful, boring even, aside from a drunk man who took exception to Joseph's cape. The Cavalier just smiled and nodded along and that only riled the drunk man, made him all red in the face and churned his blood til Annie could smell the seeth coming from his pores. A conductor came along and made him move along. The conductor was black and Annie admired his grit facing up to a white man like that. That was rarely done back then, even in so-called northern states.

"Isaac is a Jew, but not a normal Jew."
The Cavalier said that as the train pulled into Los Angeles. When A.R. asked for clarification her traveling companion looked around for eavesdroppers.
"He is a normal Jew *now*," Joseph explained, "a pillar of the Jewish community here, but in the old days he was a shootist...kind of like you but not like you; Isaac had no problem pulling his gun on someone."
That stung Annie: Even if she understood it was true the truth made her feel small.
"Now, don't smart over that," Joseph said with a gentle smile. "You don't want to be a killer. Killing someone....obviously I've never killed anyone but I have seen how it gets in a person's mind and sets ghosts loose. Not a good thing."
"This Isaac, he's killed men?"

"Yes. But do all of us a favor and do not speak of it unless he speaks of it first; it is something he has made an obsession of putting behind him."

Joseph looked out the window at the people on the platform they were coming to a stop at.

"Not that such a thing is possible," he added softly.

14

(1916)

A couple of years later, Annie would have conversations with Isaac about his take on Joseph showing up in Los Angeles like a ghost, an unwelcome one: *There is an old man here to see you, he looks like one of the Three Musketeers.* Rabbi Gould sat in his small office, hands clasped, staring down at his desk. *Why are you here, Joseph? What good could you bring?* But he knew the answer to both questions. It was a bad time for such a visit: A week earlier he had exploded during the bar mitzvah for that idiotic Fullberg boy. How was he supposed to remain calm with such a distracted boy? Now there was talk, strange looks, and it wasn't the first time. The people in his synagogue had qualms about his anger; maybe he was good for counsel, maybe he was a good leader at the Temple, but he knew that he kept them on edge.
And then the Cavalier showed up: I worried over what they could think of him? I imagined them shaking their heads and scowling: "Why is the Rabbi talking to that funny dressing Gentile?"

Isaac wanted to believe that no one knew of his past when he had come to the Temple---he was hundreds of miles away from any place where his old life had taken place. His old life had tracked him down, though.
I saw Joseph showing up as God punishing me for being so angry in the past and still being angry instead of being content with all the gifts He has given me. The rabbi assumed that God was also irritated with how Isaac missed the old days, having an excuse to ride and carry a gun and all the things he had done as a younger man. Isaac stood from his desk and felt it in his back; the aches were getting worse. He walked to a small sitting room next to his office where Joseph and Annie waited. The Cavalier stood up quickly and smiled when he saw his old friend. Isaac felt himself smiling back despite his misgivings and

the men automatically embraced. The Rabbi gave A.R. a polite smile and nod but was clearly confused as to why Joseph was traveling with a teenage girl dressed like a teenage boy.

"Joseph---how long has it been?" Isaac beamed.

"Must be twenty-five years. The beard is about half white now, I see."

"As is that mustache of yours."

They looked at each other for a few moments.

"What brings you to Los Angeles?" The rabbi asked.

"The past. I found out a couple of weeks ago that our friend passed."

"Pepe?"

"No, the Stoic."

"How could he die?" Isaac frowned. "That man seemed unkillable."

"Maybe he just got old, he was even older than us, I think."

"Quite a shame, but we all die, Joseph."

The Cavalier built a dramatic pause before looking up at his old friend with a meaningful expression.

"His bones are scattered in the desert down in Mexico, Isaac."

The rabbi saw the meaningful look on his old friend's face and didn't like it, didn't like it one bit.

I understood that he wanted us to go and collect those bones or something crazy like that. I had no problem with Joseph, Joseph I can work with, it's that old fool the Cavalier I wanted nothing to do with.

"I have an idea what you are planning, Joseph," the rabbi said with a wag of his right index finger. "And this is not a good idea."

"He saved us, Isaac---"

"Here's the thing, I am *Rabbi Gould*, now. I have responsibilities. I have a willful boy out there, somewhere, in this town."

The man in the black coat was getting angry, grit had come into his voice and into the energy around him.

"Do you have a family?" Joseph asked carefully.

The anger turned to sadness.

"My wife is dead, fourteen years now," the Rabbi said softly. "I have three children including Hershel, the one I mentioned."

"I am very sorry about Mara---"

"Joseph..." Isaac was struggling, grasping for words, trying to determine what exactly he was feeling."This is noble, this thing you want to do, but we aren't in our twenties anymore. Also, there is trouble down in Mexico---have you not heard the news about it?"

The Cavalier walked out of the room; in his place was Joseph, an aging man who had suffered a heart attack two weeks earlier.

"I understand, Isaac. I do not wish to add more burdens to our friendship so let's drop the matter."

But it was not something that either could just *drop* and the tension between them was too strong to just *vanish*.

"Why must you put me in this position, Joseph? Why have you always been the one to put me in a position where I need to make very hard decisions?"

His frustration was growing fierce; Isaac took a few seconds to compose himself.

"I have love for you, my friend, but you have always tested me. Why does it always have to be like this?"

The man in the cape looked ashamed and in turn the rabbi felt guilt; he was aware of Joseph's struggles with doubt, that his devil-may-care approach to life was a false front.

"I apologize," Joseph said quietly. "I will be in town for two days, If you want to reach me, you can leave a message at that bar a few blocks south—"

"Declan's Tavern?"

"That's the place," the man with the cape beamed.

"I do not know, Joseph, if I will be leaving you a message."

Joseph just smiled, gently clapped his old friend on the back, and left the room.

Isaac walked to his apartment in the back of the Temple, the place he hid from the house that reminded him of his wife. It had been one thing when the children had been there to distract him but now it was just the two of them: The Rabbi and his memories. In his tiny apartment, Isaac locked the front door and walked to his bedroom. The Rabbi stared at the wooden chest at the foot of his bed for ten minutes. The chest had been his since he was a boy, it had been where he kept the dime cowboy novels he had collected as a young man in New York City. The Rabbi opened the chest and pulled out a locked strongbox the size of a loaf of bread. He always kept the key on him, not anywhere a snoop could find it if they happened upon the strongbox: It was just one of the secrets he kept from the people he knew in Los Angeles but the biggest one. Isaac opened the box and pulled out something wrapped in oil cloth that he hadn't touched in fifteen years. The old man unwrapped the revolver, let the cloth fall to the floor, and turned the gun over in his hands. With a movement so fast it surprised him, the Rabbi had the revolver cocked and pointed at his bedroom door. He could feel a smile form on his face and felt guilty for it:

What was I doing? Looking at the pistol I understood that I should have disposed of it many years earlier. Holding it I timeslipped for a moment, remembered when I had drawn it on another human being. Many times I had done such a thing.

But it *felt* good, felt natural...*too* natural. Drawing the revolver had always been instinctive to him as having a gun in his hand felt natural. Life made sense when he felt his anger moving down his arm and through the old Colt. He released the hammer and wrapped the gun back up. Isaac looked over at the window and felt foolish; the blinds were open---what if someone had seen him pull the gun out and point it at the door like a crazy man? He locked the strongbox and gently set it in the trunk. He wanted to pull the gun out again, though, wanted to feel the hammer cock, maybe even dry fire it---

If there was ever one moment he could hate Joseph, that was it.

Isaac walked to the kitchen and went through the motions of making his lunch. The past, normally a vague thing that rarely came to mind, was as vivid as the present.

Was it 1885 or 1886? The last time the Cavalier talked me into his nonsense.

The gunfight had happened so fast it seemed to be over in a couple of minutes. Starn had sent six shootists he had contracted, talented men with bloody reputations. Of the four men singled out by Starn, Isaac had been the only one talented with a gun; things looked dire---

And then another shootist appeared and began firing two .45s at Starn's men, killing or mortally wounding four of them. Isaac had dispatched the other two, something that bothered him because *the act* didn't bother him: They were bad men. They deserved death; death was their business so it was only fitting.

A knock on the door brought him out of his daydreaming. The doorknob rattled and then he heard a familiar voice.

"Isaac, why is this door locked?!" Mrs Mold: She always seemed to be turning up at a bad time.

He went to the door and unlocked it. The old woman walked in shaking her head.

"Don't you have enough problems without this? You know what people will think if your door is locked."

"I know, Mrs. Mold, please."

Mrs. Mold had been the one who had helped him when he showed up in Los Angeles; she was impossibly old and stooped over.

"You have troubles, I see it," she walked over and looked hard into his face.

"Yes, but it will pass," Isaac replied.

She made a noise and waved a withered arm.

"Just tell me what it is."

"A friend from the old days visited."

Mrs. Mold's face became tight and cunning, a wise old crone. She knew of Isaac's past, maybe understood it had stayed close to his heels even when he had thought he had left it far behind.

"He has this foolish plan," Isaac continued with a shake of his head. "He wants us to track down the bones of a friend of ours."

"Bones?"

"They are down in the desert, in Mexico."

"Who was this friend of yours?"

"He wasn't a friend, just someone who saved us when we got in a bad situation." *Where I killed two men myself.*

"Sounds like an honorable thing, repaying a great debt, maybe."

"But what will happen here if I leave? I could be gone for months."

"But what if you ignore this and it eats at you? How can you lead this Temple with such a thing on your mind?"

Smelling smoke, Isaac moved to the stove and fretted over a pan.

"I was going to offer you lunch but I may have ruined it."

With some trouble, the old woman walked over to him and lay a hand on his shoulder.

"I know you, know you like none of the people who go to this Temple do. You need to take care of this or you are no good to any of us."

Isaac said nothing, but knew she was right.

15
(1957)

"How is she?"

Hector to Esmerelda as the nurse was leaving Annie's room.

"No good morning?" She asked, looking offended.

That caught the doctor off guard---was she really angry? No, the corners of her mouth were pointed up a little, betraying her.

"Weak, but she seems to be in less pain than yesterday," the nurse continued.

"I'm surprised she made it through the night," Hector said.

"The smell is worse," Esmerelda frowned. "That is a bad sign."

"Yes," the doctor agreed.

The nurse started walking away, he touched her on the shoulder and she looked back at him.

"Good morning," he added.

She smiled at him and then continued walking down the hall.

Annie was not just sitting up but sipping from her cup. The smell was worse, though, and as Esmerelda had noted it was a bad sign. Seeing Hector the patient smiled. When she moved to put the cup back on the table next to the bed there was a burst of pain and she winced.

"Here, let me get that for you," Hector said.

"Thanks, movin' pulls at my guts or something."

"Do you want to rest?" He asked.

Selfishly, he wanted her to say *no* and continue with her stories about the Cavalier and the others.

"Nah. Pull up that chair."

Once the doctor was seated, Annie continued.

"After visiting Isaac Joseph and I went to visit his friend Robert. A couple of years after our trip to Mexico I was able to visit with Robert and learn what he was thinkin' and feelin' when his old friend showed up..."

16
(1916)

The night before Joseph and Annie showed up Robert had dreamed of mountains in the desert; the Dragoons in Southern Arizona. He had been out there with Joseph and they had been much younger men. Robert had plans for the pistol he wore on his hip, plans he had made an uneasy peace with. He knew that Joseph had lied about the silver: Joseph had lied which meant he wasn't really a partner and consequently the idea of shooting Joseph down did not trouble Robert.

Robert had woken up before they found the silver. The dream had made no sense to him because he had never partnered up with Joseph nor in waking life would he ever be inclined to draw a pistol. R sat up in his fine bed which was located in one of the largest rooms in his fine house. He was no longer a young man. A hike such as the one he had dreamt of was out of the question...as was shooting another man down. How could he even dream of such a thing? What sort of murderous demon had taken over his mind in his sleep? It was troubling, but he was a busy man and forced such concerns to the back of his mind.

An hour later he was sitting alone in his dining room eating breakfast. Thoughts of the dream returned and he lost interest in his food, gesturing for the maid to take it away. He did not know her name. She was young and pretty and did not speak, that was all he knew about her. The girl was Mexican like the men who worked on the grounds. Old Mike was the only non-Mexican; the cranky colored man was so ancient that he had worked for Robert's father back east. He was pretty sure Old Mike had been a slave but the old man had no interest in talking about such things.

"You feeling poorly?" How long had Old Mike been standing there?

"Bad dream last night, about the old days."

The butler pulled up the chair nearest where Robert sat.

"I think it was in the mountains of southern Arizona, the Dragoons," the boss continued. "I was out there with this con man I knew back in New Mexico. We were out there walking around and I was hoping he would lead me to some silver he buried. Joseph, that was his name. I believe I told you about him."

"Joseph---you mean that crazy man with the cape?" Old Mike smirked.

"He wasn't crazy, just a character. A charlatan, but a good man in general."

And I was prepared to shoot him.

"When did you know him?"

"A long time ago, maybe thirty years. We never had any business together but got caught up in one situation."

Old Mike leaned forward, his elbows on the table, looking into his employer's face; he was the only one allowed to pry in his boss's affairs.

"You look awfully troubled, Robert," Mike's voice was raspy yet gentle. "Why has this gotten you bothered after so many years?"

Robert picked up his coffee cup, got it half way to his mouth, and then set it on the table.

"I have no idea."

And he wouldn't, for exactly three hours and forty minutes.

17
(1916)

It was the first motorcycle policeman either of them had ever seen; the Cavalier marveled at the sight even as the policeman asked quite curtly his business in that part of town.

"I am here to see an old friend of mine, Robert Purdue."

The policeman didn't like that. He had a stern mouth that had gotten sterner, and he was pale; how was a motorcycle cop in Los Angeles so pale?

"Mr. Purdue is a friend of Mr. Muholland's, a very important man," the policeman said sternly.

"Mr. Purdue or Mr. Mulholland?" Joseph asked.

"Are you being smart with me?" The cop took a step closer, Annie could smell his sweat and the wool of his uniform.

"No, officer, I just wasn't sure what you meant," the man in the cape continued carefully.

A lie, A.R. had seen Joseph smirking but fortunately the cop hadn't. He stepped back, looked around at the expensive houses that surrounded the three of them.

"This is a fine neighborhood," the policeman said after turning back to Joseph. "It's my job to keep characters such as yourself out of it."

More than the odors of the policemen, they could smell the oil and gasoline coming off the motorcycle in waves.

"Character?" Joseph said quietly. "I am an old man, officer."

"Maybe, but you look like one of the Three Musketeers. We don't get a lot of people dressed like you around here."

"I'm not from around here, officer."

"That comes as no surprise," Now it was the cop's turn to smirk.

"Perhaps we could telephone Mr. Purdue, he will attest to my identity."

The smirk left the policeman's face and he rested his right hand on the holster that held his billy club.

"Perhaps we shouldn't bother Mr. Purdue at all."

Fortunately for Joseph and Annie they were on the street that led from Robert's neighborhood to greater Los Angeles. As the motorcycle cop debated whether or not to use his billy club on Joseph, Robert was driving by in his Packard touring car. He instantly recognized the cape, the mustache, and the general air of a long time gadabout---

I did not have to stop. I could have just pretended that I didn't not see him and continued on my way.

But maybe he was supposed to run into his old friend, perhaps that had been the reason for the dream.

The policeman was waving for the Packard to stop so Robert did so, leaving the engine running.

"I apologize, Mr. Purdue," the cop said. "But this man says he is an old friend of yours."

All I had to do was shake my head; no words, just a shake of my head and I could have driven off and been done with the two of you.

"Yes, I do know that man."

The cop stared at Robert for a few moments: *I gave you a chance to get off the hook, pal, if you want to be bothered by your crazy friends, that's your business.*

"Very well, thank you," the policeman said deferentially.

The motorcycle cop gave Joseph one last look of disdain and then put his motorbike back in gear and rode back towards greater Los Angeles. Joseph and Robert just looked at each other for a few moments before the wealthy man reached over and opened the passenger door. Joseph looked at the motorcar warily, then forced a smile and climbed in. Annie got in the back, wary of tarnishing the fine materials.

61

"Lucky for me you passed by when you did." Joseph nodded.

"You're not colored, you would have been okay."

Why was he in Los Angeles? Did I really want to know?

Robert assumed that Joseph was there to ask for money. He would see the fine suit and even finer Packard touring car and mentally adjust the sum he desired upwards.

"You are probably wondering what I am doing in Los Angeles," Joseph said.

Robert made a show of fussing with the levers that controlled his motorcar but the Cavalier had honed in on his face, reading it, watching for signs. It made Robert uncomfortable but he said nothing.

"I am here because I heard some sad news two weeks ago," the man with the cape continued.

"Sad news? From our old town? Joseph, I cannot imagine why you would think that I had feelings for anyone in that town."

"The man known as the Stoic, the one who saved us."

Robert looked away from Joseph. His head was at such an angle Annie could not see his face but she *felt* something---pain?

"I am surprised he did not die many years ago," Robert said, his voice shaky. "He *was* a shootist."

He was trying to sound off hand but the hurt A.R. had picked up on colored his voice. Joseph was preoccupied, clearly uncomfortable riding in a motorcar. There was more than that.

When I told him of the Stoic passing...there is something I could tell you but it is not my place to, Joseph explained to Annie later. *I knew I had to turn the conversation from the dead, that it had struck Robert in a most keen fashion.*

"Must we go so fast?" Joseph said, his right hand clutching the door.

"We're barely going twenty miles per hour."

"Feels like riding greased lightning."

Annoyed, Robert dropped down to fifteen miles per hour. A man behind them in a Model T passed them and shook his fist at the Packard as he did so. "I hope you're satisfied," Robert said flatly. "We've just been passed by a Ford."

He gripped the wheel and asked a question that he understood he probably didn't want to know the answer to.

"Why are you here, Joseph? Is it just to tell me of a hired gun passing?"

Joseph was cut by the surliness in Robert's voice, he told Annie as much later on.

"It's the manner of his disposal. Pepe told me his bones were left out in the desert, that no one saw to a proper burial."

The wealthy man drove on without saying another for close to a minute.

It angered me, Joe wanted something, he always did. I was angry and then I remembered that Joseph never meant any malice, he was not an evil man; I composed myself and tried to listen fairly.

"Not to be rude, Joseph, but I am surprised at your concern. This is not something I would have thought you would give a second thought to, the welfare of another man living or dead."

Perhaps that was harsh, but it was all coming back--my dealings with Joseph in the old days. I hated how he used to smile, the joy he seemed to get when he was pulling a fast one on people. Maybe it was because he burned me a couple of times before I caught on, made me feel like a fool.

"I understand that you do not like me, Robert, never have. When I found out about the Stoic, I fell ill and nearly died, it made me look at things differently. Made me want to right some wrongs."

This made me think of the silver, A.R, Robert explained to the girl at a later date. *The dream had brought it up from the depths but I had no understanding why. Seeing Joseph reminded me of a certain hate I felt for some time that got control of me until I forced myself to bury certain memories. The man who hired guns to ambush us? He had a bag of silver stolen. Wanting to be the big man, Joseph implied that he had taken it and buried it somewhere in Mexico. Isaac was a friend of his as was Pepe, I was seen in conversation many times with Joseph arguing over debts so we all became associated with him. That was the reason we were ambushed. Seeing him and that ridiculous cape reminded me of all that...it also made me think that maybe he had taken the silver and hidden it in Mexico and was using us to help him find it under false pretenses. I have heard of men doing such things, and Joseph certainly seemed capable of such behavior.*

"I am a busy man, Joseph. I do not have the time to just go off into the middle of nowhere and peck around for bones."

Annie's friend said nothing.

Despite his silence, Robert explained to her two years later, *I was certain that Joseph was planning a clever way to drag me into his scheme, some shoddy enticement.*

"Joseph, those days are over" the driver of the motorcar added. "We're old men now, we don't have time for your nonsense."

He pulled the Packard to the curb, too upset to trust his ability to drive. Joseph looked hurt---was it an act? It didn't seem so, he just seemed a pathetic, defeated old man in a shabby costume.

"I apologize for wasting your time, Robert," Joseph said softly, holding his shoulders up in an attempt to show a pride he didn't feel. "I did not mean to offend you in any way."

The sadness seemed genuine as did Joseph's words but I could still see Joseph smirking as he buried that imaginary (?) bag of silver.

"I can give you some money if you are in need."

"I am not here for your damned money," Joseph growled, his easy smile gone. "I understand you think very poorly of me, believe I have done things that I have not, but I am not here with my hand out. I am genuinely here for the man who saved our lives and I owe a debt to, *we* owe a debt to."

He climbed out of the motorcar and looked at Robert from the curb. Joseph was so flustered that words were not coming to him.

"I apologize for upsetting you, Joseph," Robert said, gently kneading the steering wheel. "It is true that I have never seen you as a friend; despite that I do not wish you any ill will."

The harshness left Joseph's face and he smiled wearily.

"I appreciate that, Robert. I have said my peace; I will be in town a few more days, if you wish to see me for any reason Isaac will know where to find me."

He touched the brim of his hat and with Annie at his heels walked back in the direction they had come.

18
(1957)

Annie cried out in pain, and put her hands on the part of the blanket that covered her belly. Hector jumped up from his chair and went to her. Again, the patient waved him off. Her forehead was wet with sweat, the smell of heavy perspiration was mixing with the smell of bowel.

"I ain't got much time," she looked at him plaintively. "Best tell as much of this as I can."

"I can give you another shot in half an hour," the doctor said, sitting back down.

"So, this is how it ends..." Annie said quietly and then trailed off.

Was she talking to him? Hector wasn't sure. Maybe it was to the ghost of someone she had known, the doctor had experienced patients seeing ghosts in their last hours, spirits that had shown up to guide them to wherever people went when they did.

"*This is how it ends,*" the patient repeated. "I thought that the moment I realized a bullet had hit me, the moment the man across the courtyard murdered me. I saw his eyes and he saw mine; it was Macho clutching that Winchester. He understood what he had done and looked surprised and then sad. It's funny that he would help me find the job that would lead to him killing me."

She paused and looked up at the ceiling.

"I had been hearing that bullet in the air for some time. Maybe I had even been wishing for it hard enough to guide that rifle in Macho's hands. I hope you never experience what I felt before Macho killed me, doctor, when you are done with everything and feel your time has passed. I had been having those feelings in my room at night and when first waking up in the morning...feeling old and alone, like everything I had been searching for was a little too fast and a little too canny for me to find it."

Annie stopped, looked over at the pitcher of water. Hector got a glass and helped her drink a few sips.

"I would think that sitting in my plain room that always smelled of dust and old blankets," the patient continued. "That battle with Don Hector and his men was something I had been dreaming of for fifty years, slapping my holster and bringing my pistol up, being in the middle of a gunfight. It wasn't like the books or my fantasies, though."

"How long have you been in Mexico?" Hector asked. "I know you said it had been many years..."

"I came to Mexico the year President Harding died, nineteen and twenty-three," that made the patient smile but the smile was only on her face for a moment. "My mother had been ill for some years and it took her a while to die. I sold the house but there wasn't much money in that, enough to buy a good horse and travel south. Mexico was different then, still like the Old West with horses in the fields and a lack of electricity in a lot of areas. There was a feeling of wildness to the place, towns with dirt streets and no intention of paving them."

A wave of pain made her face small, she wheezed for a couple of moments, composed herself, and then continued.

"I was no longer a child but was still chasin' a fantasy; some of us never grow up, I guess. Eventually my money ran out but I knew some people and spoke Mexican by then so I got work on ranches. Not as a shootist---I do not believe I have the ice for that nor would they hire a *gringa* outsider for that---but guarding livestock on ranches. Days became weeks became years. Did my fantasy ever leave me? No. Mexico changed, tractors appeared in fields and more places got telephones and electricity. Don Miguel was even talking about getting a television, something I still am not sure about. The world had moved on but I was still standing in the same place; my heart was still in those dime novels. Once a month I would go to the nearest town and watch western movies. Even if it was all fake it still made me happy...until I left the theatre and saw electric lights in the shops and cars on the street."

The pain took over and Annie just lay there looking miserable and shifting her body trying to get some relief. Hector got another shot and administered it to his patient. Esmerelda came into the room, saw the older woman's face, and looked hurt herself.

"Poor thing," she said softly, resting a hand on Hector's shoulder as she looked over the bed.

Hector no longer saw the woman in the bed, all he was aware of was Esmerelda's hand on him.

Both the doctor and the nurse went on their rounds. Near the end of their shifts they went to see Annie together. The patient was more alert and asked the nurse to get her a glass of water.

"Thank you," she gestured for Esmerelda to take the chair.

"Remind me how you got work in Mexico," Hector said. "Not just as an outsider, but as a woman…it is quite a thing."

"It was Pepe who gave me some names in this country; folks I could give his name to as an introduction. As with Isaac and Robert, I had a few conversations with Pepe after all of us went down to Mexico. He was the last of them I spoke to before riding my horse over the border for the last time."

19
(1916)

Pepe saddled a horse and rode south. The ranch ended at three strands of barbed water broken by a plain, wooden gate. He opened the gate and kept riding. Pepe had taken care with the gate, making sure it was latched well after he had passed through; the ranch belonged to another man but it was his. It said a lot of Mr. Harmon that he entrusted his ranch to a Mexican, Pepe knew that was rare in those parts and understood that he was fortunate. When he had stopped riding with Joseph and the others, Mr. Harmon's father had given him a job at the ranch. Back then the place had been much smaller and Pepe's place on it more modest. The old man had liked him, though, saw he was honest and that he had a good head for things. Luckily, his son saw the same things and made Pepe the manager when his father had him take over the spread in 1903. What would they think of him if he rode off for weeks or months? It probably wouldn't cost him his job but it might affect his standing with Mr. Harmon and his family.

The place he found himself in was so desolate it was hard to imagine a world of cities and telephone wires and automobiles. Pepe had passed through it many times in his life, whether going back to see his family or when he had ridden with Joseph—he was in Mexico, not that the desert had any concern about nations or civilization at all; it was happy to kill you whether you were a Mexican or a *Norteamericano*. The old Mexican always got a funny feeling out there that he was between times, that it was neither 1916 or 1903 or 1885 or any other specific time in his life. Looking around, he half-expected to see Joseph and Isaac sitting on horses nearby. Pepe smiled at that thought. They had gotten lost and experienced danger, but had there been any other time he had felt so alive? The others hadn't cared that he was a Mexican, he was just another member of the gang. *The gang*---Pepe caught himself being fanciful and forced the smile off his face.

I need to remember how things ended, the shootout. Robert telling us that he thought Joseph had hidden some silver and Isaac and me insisting he hadn't. He had stood up for Joseph: Joesph was a confidence man, but he was still honest when dealing with his friends---

Was he? Is he?

Pepe opened his canteen and took a drink. There was no sound aside from the hum of insects in the sparse cholla. Had it been a mistake to tell Joseph about *los huesos*? He could have left that information out of their conversation and maybe that would have been the last time he saw his old friend. It was unusual for Pepe to get into town, normally he sent other men in his stead as the ranch kept him busy. Also, he felt comfortable there, insulated from how fast paced the world had become, taken up with its telephones and electricity and motorcars. Somewhere out there, a terrible war had been going on for two years; Pepe had heard men talking about it in town. Mr. Harmon had mentioned it, as well, but back at the ranch they had other concerns; Europe may as well have been on another planet and they liked it that way.

Even in March it was hot out on the gritty plain. Somewhere out there were the bones of *El Hombre*, the man his friends had called the Stoic. The Indian said they were scattered out there; something about that seemed shameful. He had been an honorable man---certainly had saved their lives—and deserved a proper burial, a *Christian* burial, not worthless scraps to be a prize fought over by wild animals. That thought troubled Pepe; *El Hombre* had saved them, he could have left them to be shot down but he put his own neck out and saved Pepe and the others. There had been a time during the shooting where he had, in fact, risked being struck by a bullet to save Pepe---a

Norteamerico risking his life for a Mexican. Looking out in the general direction the Apache said the bones were, Pepe had his answer. With some difficulty, he climbed back into the saddle and turned back towards the ranch.

20
(1916)

Robert was supposed to have lunch with Mullholland but canceled the
engagement over the telephone. The door to his office was closed and he had
instructed his staff not to bother him. He kept seeing Joseph's face when they
had quarreled, how hurt his old companion had looked.

*He had no right to look so indignant; he is not a man of moral standing, not
even a man who is true to his friends.*

Or was he? Was he *certain* that Joseph had hidden that silver thirty years
before? There had been so much confusion that day it was impossible to
know for sure.

Robert poured himself some whiskey and looked out the window at the
street below. He remembered how Los Angeles had been when he had settled
there, a nothing town that was the right place for a man with only ten dollars
to his name. Robert had gotten work with the Los Angeles City Water
Company, more working "in their interest" as was his way. He had met
Mullholland there and their business had become intertwined. A decade
before, it had been Mullholland that had recommended Robert buy up what
most people had been seen as worthless land. If any other man had suggested
such a thing Robert would have laughed in his face---Mullholland was not
any other man. Robert had followed his advice and it made him wealthy man
living in a fine house with indoor plumbing and electricity and not one but
three telephones. What a marvel they were, telephones and automobiles.
Now they had aeroplanes: How long would it be before you could fly from
one side of the country to the other or even to Europe? Robert hoped that he
would live to see that day. He liked all the things the new century had

brought and often wondered how they had survived in the 1800s without motorcars or electricity—

Or the telephone; good lord he loved the telephone.

When the glass was empty, Robert contemplated pouring more whiskey. He paced from his desk to the window and back again. If he drank more he understood that he would become maudlin and then nostalgic about the old days and the successful store that he had lost. The Stoic. None of the others knew exactly why the man they called the Stoic or *El Hombre* had rescued them; Robert had a pretty good idea. He and Joseph had a few conversations about their savior, Robert had even spoken of things that he had never shared with another human being. He had been nervous, anxious even, but Joseph had been kind and understanding---

And I accused him of stealing from us, that was how I repaid his understanding.

Had he ever really thought Joseph had stolen that silver or was it something else? Was it that Joseph's knowing his secret had made him dangerous to Robert? Few things are foggier to a man than his own motivations.

Robert poured more whiskey and sat at his desk. He lifted his glass in toast to the Stoic---*Noah*---and opened himself to whatever maudlin thoughts might come his way. Noah had been a man, a man just as alive as any of them and probably more, and now he was nothing more than scattered bones out in the wilderness. It seemed terribly unfair. He had been a good man, a brutal man, but still an honorable one. Noah had saved their lives, after all. Robert set his glass down and picked up the telephone. It never ceased to amaze him that he could talk to a man who was several miles away or even across the country. The telegraph had been around as long as he had but you couldn't hear a man's voice down one. What would they invent next? A way you could look at each other as you talked? They had moving pictures, maybe there was a way they could send those down wires or something. Robert gave the operator a number and a moment later he was talking to a young woman.

"Is the Rabbi available?"

"May I ask who is calling?"

"Tell him it's Robert."

"The Rabbi knows a few Roberts, sir, may I ask your last name?"

"Tell him Robert from the old days, he will know which one."

A couple of minutes passed. In that time he assessed the situation: The operator would be listening; he needed to speak with Issac in person, maybe at the Temple. Isaac seemed to know what the conversation was to be about and made the suggestion first. They agreed to meet at Robert's office where they could lock the door and speak in private.

It had been a few years since they had seen each other; their worlds did not interconnect even though Los Angeles was still---in some ways---a small town. Isaac had more gray in his beard and Robert's waist had expanded, facts the other had noted but kept to himself. The small talk lasted less than a minute as neither was a man who saw the benefit of wasting time.

"It is my understanding he came to you first," Robert said. "About the bones."

Isaac had accepted a glass of whiskey but was more savoring the way it swirled in the glass and caught the natural light than he was inclined to drink it.

"Yes. I was surprised to see he still has that cape---how is it not rags after all these years?"

"Who says it isn't?" Robert raised an eyebrow.

They both laughed at that and then felt guilty. Joseph was struggling, a sixty year old man without a place in a new suspicious world that was growing more mechanical by the day.

"Imagine us going to the wilderness to look for some bones," Isaac gestured at their bellies. "How long would we last out there now?"

"How long did we last out there then? None of us were men of the land."

And then Isaac brought up one story about the place where they had met only to have Robert bring up another.

We talked with growing excitement and fondness for a few minutes until a car backfired outside and brought us back to 1916. The room fell silent and both of us stared into our glasses.

"I don't know if he took that silver. The more I think about it...the more unsure I am."

Robert had nearly shared something with Isaac but it was a thing he wasn't sure he ever wanted to share again.

"Joseph deserved better than that," the rabbi said. "He had his faults, quite a few of them, but I am sure he didn't lie to us. Maybe he'd *embellish*, or leave out a fact or two, but he was not devious with us, not really."

Robert nodded. He had come to see that maybe he had been wrong all those years---but what of the dream he had?

"Do we do this?" He looked at Isaac plaintively. "Do we really do this?"

"I don't know. Have you heard of all the trouble down in Mexico? Could be a dangerous thing for three white men."

"Perhaps if Pepe is with us he could get us protection," Robert said.

"Do we have a way of contacting him? Do you know where he is?"

"Joseph does."

We fell into a silence that seemed to last for several minutes. To talk to Pepe we would have to talk to Joseph---we would have to be sure that we were ready to commit to going to Mexico before bringing the subject up with the man you call the Cavalier.

"This is absurd, you have the Temple and I have my affairs around here."

"Both will still be here when we get back." *If we get back.*

"Possibly." Robert thought of Noah, how he had been back then. How could such a man be killed? Age must have infermed him.

"So, do I bring Joseph here tomorrow so the three of us can talk?"

"I suppose. Maybe when the three of us are in the room together you and I will be reminded how foolish he is and it will set us straight."

I took a sip of whiskey and thought of when I had pulled the pistol out of the trunk, how good it had felt to hold it again.

"Maybe, or maybe we both have already made our decision."

21
(1957)

Annie appeared intoxicated by the morphine, smiling, apparently seeing things around the room Hector and Esmerelda were missing

"Some people knew him as The Cavalier, others simply as Joseph," the patient said. "His friends had moved on, grown prosperous while he could carry everything he owned in a couple of saddlebags..."

She trailed off, touched a few different places on the blanket that rested on her form.

"I am becoming more disconnected from my body. The funny thing is that even as something terrible is going on inside me, some death, the more at peace I am as its shadows lengthen."

"I have heard that happening to the dying," Esmerelda said then stopped. Was it wrong to tell Annie she was dying? No, it was obvious, obvious to the three of them. The patient looked up at the nurse with a gentle smile and nodded before continuing.

"Despite the calm I feel I also feel a desperation for life; being able to focus on when I was young and strong is probably an indicator that I am not as ready as I'd like to believe I am for dyin'."

Annie paused, looking at the part of the room with the most shadows.

76

"It's as clear as day, camping with the Cavalier in the wilds surrounding Los Angeles over forty years ago..."

22
(1916)

"I am not going to let this nonsense let me down."
A whisper, so quiet the coyotes in the nearby brush couldn't hear. Joseph
poked at the small campfire with a stick. Annie was nervous because there
was a house in the distance and her gut told her that they were trespassing;
back home you could get shot for such a thing. Each time she voiced her
concerns Joseph just shrugged and stared into the fire, his thoughts clearly
elsewhere. She had no idea what he was thinking; he was acting like a tired old
man when she wanted to hear more stories from *the Cavalier*. Forty years
later A.R. would see him as if he was a character in a film she was watching,
seeing his eyes and the set of his mouth and understanding things that would
take forty years and a mortal gunshot wound to understand: In the morning
he would awaken on the hard ground just as he had in his youth. The
difference was that his body would ache the next day and he would find it
hard to ignore the cold that buffered one day from the next.
"You're not happy with what your friends said, are you?" Annie asked.
A stupid question maybe, but she was desperate for conversation from him.
"It would have been foolish to expect otherwise," he nodded. "They've done
well, have responsibilities, seem to have lost the need to go on adventures.
Why haven't I lost that? Staying in one place for too long makes me
uncomfortable, the idea of a normal job is unthinkable."
Joseph smiled, poked at the fire with a stick.
"This wasn't supposed to happen."
That last sentence was almost too quiet to hear. Annie asked *what* wasn't
supposed to happen and her friend only shook his head. The girl saw
something in his face and backed off because the idea of him crying troubled
her. No, she didn't want Joseph joining them at that fire---

But he was the one staring into the flames, not the Cavalier.

This wasn't supposed to happen.

When you are sixteen it is impossible to imagine dying; you can do anything you set your mind to and nothing can stop you. When you are young and strong anything is possible---

And then you are no longer young...and then you are no longer strong.

This wasn't supposed to happen.

Getting old---that was what he meant. It would take forty years and Macho leveling a rifle at his *amiga* for Annie to understand that.

23
(1957)

"The night before Don Hector's men arrived," Annie said to the nurse. "I sat in my room thinking about how sad Joseph was as we sat next to that fire. This past winter, out on the edges of the ranchero watching for coyotes and mountain lions, I felt the cold could kill me easier than one of those beasts. What then? What would I do when I could no longer spend nights out there? I have little savings. If I went back to *el norte* there would be no Social Security for me. What then?"

The patient looked up at Esmerelda so plaintively the younger woman took Annie's left hand and in both of hers. The patient's hand was cold, too cold. The older woman gently pulled her hand away and looked over at the corner with the shadows.

"This wasn't supposed to happen," her voice was so soft it was as if she was talking to herself.

"You see," she added. "My being murdered was a blessing."

24
(1916)

The next morning Joseph sat up and felt the aches he had predicted. He said
nothing to Annie but the aches were betrayed by winces and gasps. There was
a creek nearby but it was still too cold to bathe. In the old days a bit of musk
was accepted, even expected; now that everyone had indoor plumbing a man
stood out if he smelled of living rough. Joseph walked to the creek and was
out of sight once he walked down the bank. The stream was shaded and the
water was cold as he expected. He acted blase to Annie when walking off to
clean himself but would later confess how the water had shocked him. How
had he lived like that for weeks at a time? Back at the rooming house there
was the option of a warm bath; out in the wilderness there were only icy
streams. If they went looking for *los huesos del Stoic*, this would be their life
for weeks maybe months---could he still do it?
"I'm not going to let this nonsense get me down."
Joseph said that after confessing how the cold water had gotten to him. His
voice was weak, defeated sounding. Annie could see by his face that Joseph
didn't want to be Joseph, he wanted to be the Cavalier again.
"I'm not going to let this nonsense get me down!"
The second time his voice was louder but still hollow, a weary actor playing a
part he played thousands of times and had lost the motivation for.

The walk back to town was a couple of miles. Open land became rough
double tracks that eventually became a cement road. A.R. and Joseph were
hungry, there had been some jerky and a couple of apples in her bag but they
had barely dented the travelers' hunger. For breakfast they could afford a
dime each, a quarter at the most. The majority of Pepe's "loan" had gone
towards train fare. All Joseph's friends had accepted the fate most men

81

accept, take on a real job, settle down and lead lives of solid predictability---
why hadn't he? What sort of a cushion did he have when he was too inferm
to travel and his mind too dull to charm others?

Why all the gloom, Joseph? This is a fine life, the best life; you're just
discouraged because Robert is such a sour, old fool.

Annie could see Joseph and the Cavalier battling for control on her friend's
face.

They found a small cafe that advertised breakfast for fifteen cents. The place
was half full and smelled of grease and sausages.

"You in the moving pictures?" The waitress was giving Joseph a queer look.

The man in the cape smiled his most charming smile and bowed at the waist,
the movement accentuating the ache in his back.

"No, miss, I am a traveler passing through your beautiful city."

The waitress just stared at him, openly suspicious.

"Do you have money?"

That stung---did he look that shabby?

"Yes, miss." He reached in his vest pocket and held out a dime.

On the ball, Annie fished out a dime and two nickels; they were in.

"Sit anywhere you like," the waitress said over her shoulder as she walked back
to the kitchen.

Joseph was still smiling but there was nothing behind it; A.R. had learned to
read his eyes

"All we have is sausage, eggs, and toast," the waitress called from the kitchen.

"That would be fine," Joseph replied. "Do you have coffee?"

The waitress brought out two mugs with steam coming off them.

"Are you in the theater?" She asked again.

"No, I am just a traveler," the Cavalier smiled.

"Why do you dress like that?"

"In my day, this is what a gentleman wore on the road."

"Before my time, I guess." She could have been anywhere between thirty and fifty. "What are you doing in Los Angeles?"

"Visiting a couple of old friends."

Trying and failing to get them to go on one last adventure with me.

"Do they dress like you?" The woman in the apron asked.

"No."

"Did they ever, even back in the day when you were all gentlemen on the road?"

Was it an attempt at humor? It was hard to tell, her face was expressionless and her eyes dull.

"No. People poked fun at it even then, nicknamed me *the Cavalier.*"

"To me you look like one of the three musketeers. What do your friends in Los Angeles do?"

"One is a rabbi, the other is a businessman."

"You three sound like an odd group," amusement had crept onto the waitresses face.

"Oh, back in the day we were very odd, we also had a Mexican."

"We don't like Mexicans around here," the waitress paused, looking thoughtful. "I don't know why."

"You don't know why you don't like Mexicans?"

"No, it's just something folks around here came by, I guess."

She got up to place the order with the cook. A man had walked in and sat at the counter. The waitress took his order and then walked back to where Annie and Joseph were sipping their coffee.

"Where are you two from anyway?"

"New Mexico."

"That's a long way for a visit."

"I suppose, but I had a good reason. It's a long story, though."

She was looking at Joseph expectantly so he told her about the bones and how the Stoic had saved the four of them thirty years earlier.

"Golly, a real gunfight," her face had come to life, she looked impressed. "You're the first person I've ever talked to who has been in one."

"It is a terrifying experience, I'll tell you. I don't know if I was more scared of getting shot or shooting another man."

"Have you ever shot another man?"

"Accidentally," Joseph replied. "I was trying to scare him by shooting close but I hit him, thank God it was not a mortal wound."

"I'm sorry your friends don't want to go with you, it sounds like quite an adventure."

"Yes. Maybe we're too old for adventures, though, maybe this whole idea was foolish."

The waitress looked down at Joseph with what appeared to be genuine kindness.

"Maybe," she said thoughtfully. "Nevertheless this man who saved you, he sounds like an honorable fella."

"He was."

"It'd be a shame if he didn't get a Christian burial."

"I agree."

She looked at him meaningfully then went to get their food.

25
(1916)

Joseph got to the doors of the Temple but couldn't find it in himself to knock. He stared at it for a few moments, and then paced the sidewalk in front of the building; it was just a door and yet it wasn't. Annie stood nearby, trying to figure out why Joseph had taken over; he had been asleep in the diner, the Cavalier regaling the waitress with all sorts of stories, but now the Cavalier had disappeared leaving a doubtful old man in his place. Isaac had admired him, almost been a sidekick---(a word the rabbi used in one conversation with Annie)---and now he was an important man in his community, a man who had matured and gotten stature. Joseph probably felt the weight of his shabby cape and all his decisions over the years; light one by one but in the millions unbelievably heavy. The door to the Temple opening startled him. Isaac was staring at him from the other side, he looked angry.

"This is fortuitous, we have been talking about you and your scheme."

"It is not a scheme, Isaac, not this time."

The rabbi just stared for a couple of moments then his expression softened.

"You know, I look at your face and I believe you," Isaac said gently.

Joseph looked at the open doorway Isaac was still blocking.

"I remember the first time I met you, you had just killed a man."

Isaac looked around and then at Joseph with a ferocious shaking of his head.

"You cannot say things like that around here. In fact, you cannot say them at all."

"I'm sorry---"

"I am not that person anymore, I can't be."

Looking at the rabbi you could tell that, despite his advancing years and attempts at civility, he was still that young man with a gun. They looked at each other, both seeing a lie and choosing to ignore it.

"Come into my office: I will telephone Robert and then we can talk."

Two hours later, the three of them were sitting in a rabbi's office drinking coffee. Annie felt like an outsider and kept to a plain chair near the wall. Isaac was kind, though, and offered her coffee just as he had the others. Robert had the money and seemed to believe that put him in charge of the expedition.

"I can arrange for a truck or two to use on the search," he said.

"There are no roads where we are going," Joseph pointed out. "We will need horses and mules."

"I have heard that cars do fine in the open desert," The wealthy man said dismissively. You just have to watch for sand."

"Perhaps, but there are also mountains," Joseph countered. "It sounds like the bones are up in the hills a bit...."

Robert made a face and shifted uncomfortably in his chair.

"Are you proposing we make this trip on horseback? Look around the room, Joseph, we are not young men."

"Perhaps we can bring a car along," Isaac suggested. "We can have both horses and a motorcar. I mean, there have to be *some* roads in Mexico."

Joseph had his doubts but said nothing; Robert was clearly on the verge of jumping ship. He also understood that his position was a weak one as he depended on the others to buy any provisions they would need. Annie assumed that her friend felt humbled and nostalgic for the days when they were all on equal ground. Now, in the space of a year that amount of money that passed through his hands probably couldn't even buy one of Robert's suits.

It took two days to contact Pepe at the ranch. There weren't any phone lines out there; a telegraph had to be sent to the nearest town and then a runner sent out to the ranch. Isaac offered Joseph and Annie cots in the Temple but his friend said that they had a "fine camping spot" and politely declined.

We watched you and Joseph walk off, Isaac told A.R. two years later. *His cape fluttered a bit and it was painful to see; an old bird who can't fly anymore. Robert shook his head, I ran my finger along the scalloped edge of the cup that I had been drinking from.*

"What is going to happen to him?" Isaac mused, as much to himself as Robert.

"I have no idea. It's amazing to me that a sixty year old man can still be attached to the life he led as a young man."

"Are you still thinking he stole that silver?"

"I don't know," Robert looked into his cup. "Why would he lead such a threadbare life if he had?"

Isaac's arm had started aching, he stretched it to get the kinks out.

"I don't think he had any part in taking that silver," the rabbi said. "I think he got to bragging and it led to bad things."

Both of them were silent for a few moments before Robert spoke.

"Obviously someone believed we took it."

"I don't know," Isaac replied. "Maybe there was another reason Jason Starn wanted us dead."

I gave Robert the sort of look that means more than words can. He said nothing but averted his gaze and then walked over to the window. There are things about Robert, things I am not sure I will ever come to terms with, things that even after thirty plus years confuse me. Confusion has never sat well, feels like a form of weakness, and my own weakness often stirs my anger.

"Why would Jason Starn, brother of Matthew Starn, want us dead?" The rabbi added.

"You're saying the ambush was my fault?" Robert asked with the beginnings of anger.

Knowing making accusations served no positive purpose, Isaac backed down.

"Who knows," he said softly.

"I would hope that you could refrain from making assumptions regarding my business in the future."

The rabbi looked up at his friend with a sad smile.

"Nothing would make me happier, Robert."

26
(1916)

A.R. and the Cavalier wandered the neighborhoods until twilight when they passed a church. The man in the cape motioned for her to follow him to and through the front doors; no one else was inside.

"A pew makes a poor bed, A.R., but it will be better than hiking out into the country and sleeping on the ground."

The cavalier sat on a bench nearest to the pulpit in such a way that it would look like he was praying if anyone walked in---maybe he was. There was an odd heaviness in his chest and more and more often he would find himself short of breath, something he would share with his friend later on.

"I was surprised to see anyone in here."

The voice belonged to a bald priest somewhere in his mid-fifties. He looked familiar to Joseph but he couldn't place the familiarity.

"I have many things on my mind, Father," the Cavalier said, doffing his hat. "I came in here to see if the good Lord could help me with my reflections."

The priest sat down on the far side of the pew and looked at the pulpit.

"You look like a man on an adventure," he said.

There was something in the timbre of his voice, an edge not belonging to a fellow of the cloth.

"I suppose I am," the Cavalier agreed. "My friends and I will be leaving for Mexico in a few days."

The priest looked over at his guests, he was smiling but it was a cold smile that made Annie uneasy: *He knows Joseph, knows him and doesn't like him.*

"Mexico," the priest said. "I have heard that it has become a dangerous place."

"Perhaps, but we have a debt that we need to repay. An old friend died down there and was left out in the elements without a proper burial. We mean to find his bones and see they are given a proper, Christian burial."

The priest said nothing for nearly a minute.

"I envy you; I am so busy with this church I haven't been out of Los Angeles--even this neighborhood--for years."

The Cavalier chuckled amiably and gestured with his hat towards the front doors.

"Always room for one more, Father."

They smiled at each other and Joseph felt certain that they would be offered cots.

Oh, the will to survive and the dark streets it leads us down.

He said that to A.R. on the train ride back to New Mexico when they talked about their time in that church.

"Tell me about this debt, Mister---"

"Seller, Joseph Seller. Well, there was a misunderstanding around thirty years ago. A powerful man thought that we had robbed him---"

"Did you?" The priest asked sharply, taking a step closer to Joseph.

"Pardon?"

"Did you rob him?" The father's tone had become harsh.

"It doesn't matter," Joseph sighed. "His money had been stolen from the weak, he was a foul person, a thief in a waistcoat. I did things back then that I am not proud of but my deeds were hardly worthy of hiring shootists to gun us down. This man had us ambushed; we surely would have perished if not for a gunman with skills best described as miraculous."

The priest took another step towards Joseph, Annie could see that his body had become as tense as his face.

"This ambush, did it take place in 1886 in Deming, New Mexico territory?"

"Yes, Father."

Joseph could smell something unfortunate in the air, the cot he thought was his vanishing in the ether.

"Am I to assume the *thief in a waistcoat* was named Jason Starn?" The priest asked.

"You know him?" Joseph's smile had faded sensing the game he had been playing was turning against him.

The priest turned to Joseph with naked contempt.

"He is my older brother."

Joseph just looked at the priest and nodded his head as if to acknowledge that God had just played another practical joke on him.

"My," he said weakly. "This old world gets smaller by the week."

"You and your friends are going to hell!" The priest yelled. "Especially Robert Purdue!"

Joseph and Annie rose from their pews and gathered their bags.

"Perhaps, Father Matthew, but at least we do not hide our darker selves in the costume of a priest."

Father Matthew turned his hands into fists---would he attempt to strike the intruder?

"I earned this, sir, I made amends for my sins long ago. And you know nothing about my brother; he paid for this church and several others, he had donated millions to charities---what have you done? What has your relationship with your fellow man been aside from manipulation and petty theft?"

Joseph looked stunned, wounded, but he managed to become the Cavalier again.

"I will take my leave now, Father," he said with another doff of his hat. "Good day to you."

The two intruders walked out of the church. The priest did not send any further words towards their backs. It was dark by that point and the Cavalier and A.R. had the understanding that they would be sleeping rough again.

The cops in Los Angeles clearly did not like the down and out; Annie and the Cavalier would get settled on a park bench only to get rousted ten to fifteen minutes later: The old man wearing a cape stood out but so did the girl wearing boy's clothes. Growing more weary as the night grew in hours, the two of them wandered into the colored part of town. Finding a small park, Joseph sat on a bench and stared out into the darkness. Annie sat on the grass a couple of feet away.

"Someone is watching us." His voice was a cat slowly moving out from a safe place, a secret thing wishing to remain invisible.

"You don't say," A.R. responded; she hadn't seen anyone.

"Yes, across the park. I guess my old instincts have been coming back."

She was impressed as, even glancing around a second time, Annie saw nothing. The Cavalier gestured for the invisible person to join us. It was a colored boy, somewhere around ten. The child walked from the shadows and into the yellow light. He looked intelligent beyond his years, unafraid.

"Hello, there." The Cavalier said warmly, touching the brim of his hat and smiling with what appeared to be genuine joy.

The boy did not smile, he just continued staring.

"You don't live around here, do you?" The child asked.

"No, we are travelers. Name is Joseph, my friend is A.R."

"You're a girl, right?" The boy frowned at Annie.

"Yes."

"Why are you in boy's clothes?"

"Like 'em, I guess. You got a name?"

"I'm James, but my folks call me Jimmy. We've only been here a few months; Daddy came out for work."

"You like it here, James?" The Cavalier asked.

The boy seemed pleased that Joseph had used his proper name.

"It's fine, I guess. I found some boys to play ball with."

"Ball? You mean stick ball?"

"No, basketball. We ain't fancy, we just use an ol 'peach basket but it works fine."

The Cavalier looked over at Annie with a wink before turning back to the child.

"I've heard of basketball but never seen it played, maybe I'll have to watch you and your friends play sometime."

"You'll probably be gone before tomorrow," Jimmy nodded wisely. "Cops will probably make you scoot."

"Maybe," The man in the cape agreed.

"Jimmy? You out here?" A man's voice, deep and worried.

A heavyset colored man emerged from the shadows. He looked from the boy to the Cavalier and Annie with suspicion before focusing on his son.

"You git on back to the house, hear?"

"Yes, Daddy," James said reluctantly before nodding at the strangers. "Nice to meet you Joseph and A.R. We'll be playing in this park tomorrow if you're still here."

"If I am, I will definitely watch you boys play."

Jimmy smiled a dazzling smile and then turned and walked back into the darkness. His father sat on the bench next to Joseph.

"You ain't from around here, are you, sir?"

"Nope, just a traveler, as I told your son. I tried to get some rest in some other parks, but the police made me scoot."

That made their new acquaintance sad or bitter or maybe both.

"They'll do that, especially to a colored man or a Mexican."

Joseph nodded and looked across the dark grass.

"I imagine. Fine boy you got there."

The mention of his son didn't make the man happy, if anything he looked more troubled.

"He can be, but we've had problems."

"Oh?" Joseph asked, turning the other man on the bench.

"Shouldn't talk about it, family business."

"I understand."

The man rose from the bench and extended his hand.

"Nice to meet you. I'd offer you a place in our house, but it's full as it is."

"I understand, very kind of you anyway."

The man stood, walked a few steps into the darkness, and then turned back towards the travelers.

"If you need a meal in the mornin', Cecilia's is two blocks that way. They don't get many white folk so tell them that you know Clarence Dube."

"Will do, much obliged."

Clarence walked back to Joseph. The man in the cape stood up and the two of them shook hands.

"Good night, sir," Clarence said with a smile.

"Good night to you, as well."

Clarence Dube turned and followed his son into the darkness.

27
(1957)

Neither Hector nor Esmerelda wanted to leave Annie at the end of their shifts; she seemed close to the end and would probably be dead by the time they clocked in the following morning. Both Mexicans were surprised to see that she had rallied, and was even eating some soft food when they checked on her.

"How did your mother react after you ran away?" The nurse asked.

Annie smiled and stopped eating.

"My going to Los Angeles with the Cavalier was the last straw for her. When we returned from Mexico I had no choice but to head to Los Angeles. Isaac gave me odd jobs to do around the temple but since I wasn't a Jew I couldn't stay there or anything like that. The two of us talked a lot, though."

She stopped to spoon some more food in her mouth. Swallowing appeared to cause her pain.

"I thought I had lost a lot of those memories but they keep coming back," she said softly, almost to herself.

Annie handed the bowl to Esmerelda who set it on the nightstand.

"It sounded like you became close with Isaac," the nurse said.

"Yes," the patient looked happy at that thought. "He became a sort of father to me. My own pa, he had died of snakebite when I was really small. The rabbi was very secretive at first, but eventually he started telling stories of when he and Joseph met."

She motioned for water. Hector filled a cup and handed it to Esmerelda who helped the patient drink.

"Isaac asked me, out of the blue, if I remember when Joseph had mentioned that when they had met, Isaac had just killed a man. I said I did. Well, the rabbi looked so sad I took one of his hands, tried to comfort him. I told him it had been a long time ago and that he should let his guilt go."

The happiness had left Annie's face, she looked into the nurse's eyes.

"Isaac told me that he didn't feel guilt and that was what troubled him. What sort of a man could gun another human being down and feel absolutely nothing?"

28
(1882)

The man had been coarse, cruel even, taunting Isaac by calling him a *dirty Jew*. Isaac had also seen the fellow beating on a mentally feeble man and mistreating a horse; shooting him had been easy just as it had been with the other men he had gunned down. It had been unclear if the man had been reaching for his sidearm but Isaac wasn't taking chances. He fired two, the man gurgled and rasped,, made a terrible face and fell to the ground. A few moments later the man on the ground changed and Isaac guessed that he had died and his spirit had left him. People came out of the shops and saloons to see what had happened. A few doors down, a man with a rifle emerged from a building, probably the law---*hopefully,* seeing as Isaac was a stranger and a Jew at that. A fellow around his age in a bright blue cape approached him, hands away from his sides and in plain sight.

"You'll want to act a bit more shaken up when the law gets here," the stranger nodded. "You're a bit too cool, my friend."

Isaac's advisor wore a strange hat like one of the musketeers and was smiling wisely and nodding almost hypnotically. The killer wasn't shaken up, he was ready to shoot again if needed; maybe the man lying in the dirt had friends ready to take revenge.

"I need you to holster your sidearm, son."

An old man with a rifle stopped off to Isaac's right, his voice was gentle but firm.

Isaac did as he was told, making his hand shake a little as instructed.

"I saw it all, sheriff." The man in the cape said loud and clear. "The dead fellow was reaching for his sidearm and this young man was defending himself."

"Is he dead?" The sheriff asked a man who was standing next to the body.

"Reckon; he ain't movin' and some of his brains leaked out of his head."
The sheriff turned to the man in the cape.
"What is your name, sir?"
"Joseph Gamble of Kansas City, sheriff."
And Joseph was off: Taking charge of the situation, distracting the sheriff enough that he no longer cared or was too worn down to bother with the details of the shooting.

"Do you have affairs to tend to in this town?"
Joseph asked the shooter that as they were walking out of the sheriff's office where details of the incident had been recorded.
"No, I have a room for the week, but otherwise, no."
Joseph nodded, looking up and down the street as he did so.
"That fellow you shot, he has people somewhere. His accent was local so I'm guessing they are not more than a day or two from here. I believe it would be in your best interest to leave this area as soon as possible."
Isaac no longer felt like a cool gunman, he felt out of his element and possibly surrounded by danger.
"Where should I go?"
Joseph smiled at him; over thirty years later Isaac could still recall how generous the smile was.
"You can ride with me," Joseph offered. "You said you're from New York--what does your father do?"
"He's a rabbi in our temple."
"Don't meet many Jews out here. Personally, I have always enjoyed the company of Hebrews. How long have you been on the road?"
"A few months."
Joseph nodded and seemed to be processing the information he was receiving.

"What led you to leave an exciting place like New York for all this?"
Boredom. Questioning whether he wanted to be a rabbi like his father---
many reasons, none he had shared with Joseph; not then, at least. Thirty-four
years later, he was turning the same revolver he had shot other men with over
and over in his hands as he told the story of the shooting to Annie. People
had seen Joseph as a fool or an eccentric, given him the nickname *the
Cavalier* because of his clothes, but Joseph seemed to see everything and
understand people like no other man Isaac had ever met. He could have been
a great man but had followed a different road.

"It was his own road, at least," Issac had admitted in 1918.

The memories had put him on the verge of tears so Annie asked no further
questions.

29
(1957)

"Why didn't you stay longer in Los Angeles?" Hector asked.

Esmerelda looked at him as if he were foolish.

"She said it was boring, didn't you hear that?" The nurse asked.

Hector looked embarrassed but even when she scolded him, he enjoyed when she talked to him, any interaction.

"Los Angeles was a place where Trouble and I took to each other's company," Annie said. "Eventually I did something stupid and returned to New Mexico to avoid jail. I never saw Isaac nor Robert again. I'm certain they've passed by now.

The rabbi worked all the time to keep the man he was---the man he *really* was---closed up in a secret room. I have no doubts that he believed that he could change up to the day he died."

Another wave of pain, the patient grimaced but again waved the nurse away when Esmerelda reached over to comfort her.

"You guys are good together," Annie said weakly. "You ought to follow that path both of you are looking down."

Seeing the embarrassment on their faces, the dying woman continued.

"Robert's situation was more complicated; it seemed that he understood he had no interest in changing but still had a healthy amount of self-loathing. I never could get enough of their stories about the old days. Isaac would invite me to his office and share the stories but in them it was like the old him was another person, a fictional character almost. Robert had no such delusions. He would have me sit on a cheap chair in his study and sip brandy that was never offered to me.

1885, that had been the year I first crossed paths with Isaac and Joseph. Joseph had been running some scheme that had to do with double selling barbed wire or something like that. I had been running my father's store and Joseph had utilized the store in his plan.

30
(1885)

In the middle of the whole scheme some hayseed had figured out that he was being taken for a ride and word spread that he and his family meant to lynch Joseph and Isaac. The hayseed was well known and liked in the area, unlike the strangers who had been in town barely a week. Robert, on the other hand, had been fascinated by them: A young man who looked like a rabbinical student and a fellow in a cape and swashbuckler's hat. He has grown bored with Purdue Mercantile. Running the store was something he did well but Robert was 27 and felt too young to be stuck with it. Impulsively, he went up to the room the strangers were renting. Robert had seen them as harmless con men and had been caught off guard when Isaac pulled his pistol on him; he *looked* like a young rabbi but his eyes were cold. You could see that he had used that pistol before and had no problem using it again.

"You can put that away," Robert said, trying to sound cool. "I am a friend."

Joseph had smiled at Robert and touched his companion's shoulder. Isaac reholstered the pistol without taking his eyes off Robert.

"It looks like we will be leaving town straight away," the man in the cape had said to his companion.

"I didn't even say a word, mister," Robert said, suddenly anxious that his opportunity to escape that dull town and his father's dull town was being taken away from him.

"You didn't have to, I know why you're here," Joseph said calmly. "I've seen your face many times over the past several years."

"Which direction are you riding in?" The visitor asked impulsively.

Joseph just laughed a little.

"Please, friend; you know I can't tell you that."

The door to escape had clearly slammed shut. Robert firmed up and backed towards the door.

"Fair enough," he said. "I just thought I should warn you, people only a few hours from here will be riding out to settle things."

Joseph and Isaac rode off and eventually ended up in Deming. The Cavalier ran his schemes but with greater caution and skill. Eventually Robert had a falling out with his folks for reasons he never shared with Annie. A fellow he knew ran a dry goods store in Deming, Robert bought in and soon grew reacquainted with the Cavalier and Isaac. They weren't friends, just knew of each other and saw each other around town. Robert picked up that Joseph understood people like no other man he had ever met. Isaac was a human contradiction: A religious man, a well read man, but also a man who could kill as easily as a fellow could eat an egg. Isaac had been reading dime cowboy novels since he was a boy, saving his money to secretly buy his pistol. The boy had taught himself to shoot in a place called Central Park. During the day he would study the Talmud and at night go out to the park and shoot. He found out that he was a natural---all these details came out over weeks and months that Isaac would appear in the shop to buy this or that. Joseph told stories that may or may not have been true. Isaac was more earnest and told of his life, how he had grown restless about seeing all the places he had read about in the flimsy novels.

31
(1916)

Robert stared at the luggage stacked in his bedroom, understanding that he had packed too many bags. He recollected how it had been riding day after day and felt doubt about the whole undertaking. It wasn't the first time such feelings had cast him an elbow in the ribs.

I'm 58, my bowels aren't what they used to be, this is stupid.

On the other hand he couldn't deny that the idea excited him: He had been feeling something undefined and yet familiar the past couple of years--- boredom. Robert had contemplated visiting Europe but then the War had broken out. There was always Asia but those people had strange ways he couldn't get a handle on; strange food, as well. There were problems with every destination a civilized man with money was supposed to see in his lifetime. Maybe that was the problem, maybe he *wasn't* a civilized man, money or no money. He had run the Purdue Mercantile with honesty and directness but there had always been something else in his heart, an unfamiliar voice suggesting that there was something waiting for him down roads he had never traveled.

32
(1916)

A crowd of toughs had called a man names and gave him quite a licking---that was the only thing Annie could recall about the train ride from Los Angeles to Deming. The four of them had stopped at some town and were looking out the windows of the train at the platform. A group had gathered, one man surrounded by others as they yelled at him. The surrounded man looked scared and had a good sized mustache. The Cavalier got close to the window and pressed his hand against it. It was easy to see that the scene was making him anxious.

"Why are they treading on that fellow?" He asked his companions. "It seems like he's in for a beating---doesn't he have a friend out there?"

Isaac was also watching through the window but instead of anxiety he felt something else, something harder. An expression A.R. had not seen on his face before.

I could see Joseph wanted to do something for that poor fellow. He was agitated but not quite ready to put his old body in the way of the bullies. The man I have tried to kill was getting stronger---I did not tell the rest of you but my pistol was in the bag I had at my feet. The man who I had tried to kill was suggesting I take that pistol and go defend the man about to be beaten.

A conductor was coming down the aisle. The Cavalier turned from the window and got the attention of the conductor.

"Say, do you know why they are yelling at the poor man?"

The conductor looked out the window and sneered.

"He's a kraut, sir."

"Kraut?"

"A German."

"We are not at war with Germany, not yet, at least."

104

The conductor put hands on his hips that became fists. Annie could smell his sweat and the meat he had eaten for breakfast as he leaned over her to address the Cavalier.

"The Huns are evil, sir. A wise man would not be standing up for them on this train."

He gave Joseph one last stern look and then continued down the aisle. The German man had left the platform---had the crowd dispersed or simply followed him into town to dole out their punishment? It was easy to see that Joseph was torn as to what to do, he later told Annie as much.

As gentlemen we should have made sure that fellow was not molested, but I understood that our union was tenuous and such an action could have unraveled it altogether. That was a logic explanation for why I did not lead a charge to help that fellow but was it the real reason? Was I really concerned for our mission to do right by the man who had saved us, or was I just protecting my silly, old hide?

The train began to move, the party remained in their seats.

33
(1916)

Pepe met them at the train station in Deming. The four men took a couple of minutes to look his companions over from man to man. Even the three that had traveled together were clearly seeing something they hadn't now that they were back in the place where they had been young and more open to making mistakes. No one else on the platform existed, Annie included.

"How did we get so old?" Joseph, his tone wistful.

The girl saw some grit drift across Pepe's normally kind face.

"We can't think that way," he said firmly. "We need to think about *El Hombre*, why we are doing this."

Pepe looked in the general direction of Mexico as if to underline his point.

"I think we should get a drink to celebrate our being together." Isaac, looking around for a bar. "There's a saloon over there."

"That one does not let Mexicans in." Pepe, mostly sad.

"Some things never change." Robert shaking his head.

"I know a place, a Mexican place."

"Will they serve the three of us? What about A.R.?"

"The only color they care about is *verde*."

"Como debería ser," Robert said---*as it should be.*

Four Mexican boys were standing nearby, looking to Pepe for instruction. He turned to them, rattled off something in Spanish, and then turned to his guests.

"I am having them take the baggage to your hotel."

"Gracias, muchachos," Joseph, turning to the boys as he touched the brim of his hat.

The boys giggled at this and then went to attend to the luggage.

On the walk to the bar, Isaac couldn't help but notice how Pepe waddled a little and Robert wheezed.

And we were thinking of going out into the wilderness? Us?

"It was here." Pepe had stopped next to a building that was one of the oldest in town.

The others stopped, looked around, and realized he was right. Thirty years had passed but the memory was vivid for all of them.

"I remember the wood on that post splintering when the bullet hit it," Robert said.

"Yes, you can see where the wood is damaged," Isaac smiled.

Unconsciously, each man was gravitating to where he had taken cover. Most of the places had changed and passers-by were watching them in curiosity: Four old men wandering into the street, seeming oblivious to the cars and trucks.

"I was pinned in over here," Pepe gestured towards what was now a general store. "All the bullets seemed focused on me; I thought I was going to die."

"Funny, I was thinking the same thing," Joseph said with a thoughtful expression.

Isaac remained silent. Unlike his companions he had not felt fear or confusion.

I felt a clarity, an understanding of what needed to be done. Unlike the others, there was no hesitation or doubt when I drew my pistol, no concern of harming another human being.

His shots were purposeful and only two bullets were wasted before one of the shooters cried out in agony and fell. The wounded man's companions, all experienced and skillful men, realized Isaac was their only true adversary and focused their fire on him. He took on too much fire to shoot back without exposing himself and the other three were not skillful enough to provide him cover---

And then the Stoic came riding down the street. The grace of his actions stunned the men on both sides of the gun battle: One moment he was riding and then next he was off his horse and taking cover as he withdrew a sidearm from its holster. He emptied one pistol and then withdrew a second. By the time the second revolver had spent four shells, the ambushers were all dead or mortally wounded, two due to Isaac's actions.

The four men were startled out of their recollection by a car horn and some vulgar shouting by the man driving it.

"The bar, it's down this street here," Pepe said, waving at the man in the car.

"Yes, we should get off the street before we're struck down," Robert agreed.

Isaac followed the others but felt uncomfortable having his back to the rooftops where the ambushers had been shooting from; Annie could tell by his face that it was no longer thirty years in the past. The cantina was a dim place heavy with the smell of body odor. The man behind the bar wore an enormous mustache and looked suspicious at the gringos walking in. Pepe went up to him and spoke in Spanish. The bartender spoke harshly at first but whatever Pepe was saying to him calmed him and in the end the bartender nodded and smiled grimly.

"Please, sit at any table you like,: the bartender called across the room in a high pitched voice. "I will bring you out a bottle and some glasses."

The ranch manager rejoined his companions.

"What did you say to him, Pepe?" Joseph asked.

"I said that you gentlemen were a thorn in Jason Starn's side."

"And that did the trick?"

"Senor Starn is not a good name around here; he is notorious for how he treated the Mexicans who worked in his mines."

"Is there going to be any trouble for us over the border?" Robert, preoccupied by two Mexicans who had just walked in and were scowling in the direction of their table.

"I don't know," Pepe said thoughtfully. "Some will see the honor in what we are doing, others will just see you as gringos to rob or kill."

"Rob or kill." The Cavalier's tone was unusually subdued.

The others looked at him and he realized that it was up to him to rally them, to keep them motivated on their adventure.

"To the Stoic," Joseph smiled as he raised his glass. "He saved us and now we are repaying the debt."

The rest of them raised their glasses and echoed the toast. Annie had never drank whiskey before and after the sip she took it would be another several years before repeating the mistake.

"Maybe we should practice with our sidearms, we're probably rusty," Robert suggested.

"We weren't any good to begin with," Pepe smiled.

"Except Isaac," the Cavalier pointed out.

The three of them looked across the table at the rabbi who shrugged and then took a drink.

"It doesn't matter," the rabbi shrugged. "If they come at us it will be dozens of men. Even if all four of us were skilled with a gun, we'd be severely outmatched."

Joseph felt the mood darkening giving second thoughts a chance to bloom.

Why am I dragging them into this, anyway? Just because I need this?

"Listen, if any of you want to back out I understand. I will just require a loan to provision myself---"

"Don't be ridiculous." Isaac, pouring more whiskey into his glass. "I'm going, that's final."

"We would be dead without *El Hombre*." Pepe sighed.

Robert remained silent. He was tired and his bowels had been troubling him. *And now we will be riding for weeks without a proper bathroom or restaurant or any sort of comforts?*

But then he thought about Noah, the man he had known and been friends with. He thought of him alive and then considered his bones out there scattered in the grit. The others were looking at him, the table had fallen silent.

"I will see about arranging a car and some gasoline," he said. "I am determined to stay off a horse as much as possible."

His companions looked at him then at each other again. Sips of whiskey were taken, a minute passed in comfortable silence.

"Do you remember Abel, Joseph?" Pepe asked.

"Yes, he seemed like a good man, an old timer like us."

"I would like to bring him along to help us with the day to day things, cooking, taking care of the horses."

Pepe looked around the table, no one seemed opposed to the idea.

34
(1916)

The road from Deming faded into the desert a few miles south of the border. Two faint tracks were all that remained, seeming to stretch on forever into the hostile landscape.

"It may as well be the 80s; this place never changes."

Robert sighed as he said that, shaking his head before putting the car back in gear and driving on. Abel rode in the front seat beside him; the rest of the car was full of provisions. The other four rode alongside on horses. The old men engaged in nostalgia as they poked along at the walking speed of the horses, speaking of the ways the world had changed since the time of their youth.

"Most of the motorcar drivers are madmen, people in my temple are always having close calls," Isaac shook his head.

"It's still a new thing, people need to get used to them," Robert replied.

"Maybe, but how many people will die before that happens?" Isaac scowled.

Robert said nothing in response. He had no time for people who refused to embrace progress.

"I remember the first time I saw an automobile," Joseph said wistfully. "It was before the new century by a couple of years. That machine was quiet as a ghost, nearly scared the tar out of me."

"Must have been an electric one," Robert said. "Were you in a city?"

"Yes, New York City, in fact."

"Never knew that you had been to New York," Isaac said.

"Just once."

"I imagine it has changed a lot since I left." Now it was Isaac that sounded wistful.

"You've never been back?" Robert asked.

"A few times, but only for short visits."

Pepe kept looking over his shoulder in the general direction of the Harmon ranch.

I had left an older hand named Sebastian in charge. Sebastian was smart, a good man, and that worried me. What if Mr. Harmon liked having Sebastian in charge? What if he realized he was more comfortable having a white man looking after the place rather than a Mexican?

Pepe, riding at the back of the group, seemed to be watching Joseph's cape as it fluttered behind him; it reminded Annie of folks who watch birds. Sometime after they returned from Mexico she asked him about it.

Even from twenty feet that old cape looked shabby---I was following a shabby man away from everything that was good for me and my family. And then Joseph looked over his shoulder and smiled at me; I felt bad for having those thoughts about one of my friends. I should have been focused on what I knew was a sacred duty: El Hombre had saved us. We were doing the right thing. That was all that mattered.

The tracks lead down into a narrow valley. All of them looked up at the escarpments towering over the group and felt nervous---no one said as much, but each of them could see concern on their companions' faces. The Apache were supposedly gone but there were revolutionary Mexicans looking to shoot white men.

"I hear some Apaches are still holed up down here," Chokes seemed to be regretting his decision to join them. "Some of the Mexicans at the ranch say that, even today, bands of them are hiding in hills like those up there."

"The Apache are gone."

The Cavalier said that with elaborate confidence. A.R. knew his voice by then, though, and she picked up on Joseph's doubt. The Apache had been subdued even before the Stoic had saved them---subdued, but not eradicated.

Not the fiercest of a proud, iron tough tribe. Like the others, the Cavalier had feared the Apache but had respected and even admired them. A couple of tears had even made their way down his face when news came of Geronimo's end.

"It's a shame, really." Issac's voice was soft. "I remember in my novels they were these bloodthirsty demons. In Central Park I would pretend trees were Apaches or Cherokees before shooting them. The first real Indians I saw were on a reservation, they looked like broken people...."

He started getting choked up and trailed off, shaking his head as if the memory were a pest on his skin.

"I remember that story," Joseph smiled. "When I was in New York I went to Central Park looking for trees with bullet holes. I stopped when I realized that many men must have done the same thing."

"Not in New York City. I could have gotten in a lot of trouble if I hadn't been dressed like a rabbinical student."

"That must have been quite a sight," Robert said.

"I saw a policeman watching me a couple of times. He just stood there, maybe a couple hundred feet away. Maybe he didn't have a gun, I have no idea why he didn't confront me."

Isaac twisted the reins over one hand and then untwisted them, focusing on the feel of the rawhide on his skin.

"Those novels were garbage," he growled. "Nothing more than propaganda."

No one had a response to that, they rode on, still keeping an eye on the escarpments.

"Would you be satisfied if we had left them be?" Robert, his tone unreadable.

"The bones?" Isaac asked.

"Yes."

"That's an impossible question, like asking what my life would be like if I had stayed in New York."

"Looks like a village up ahead." Chokes, sensing the tension and trying to break it.

"Los Huesos."

Chokes didn't like what he heard in Pepe's voice when his boss said the name of the village. He didn't know what *Los Huesos* meant---he didn't speak much Mexican, said that many times with almost touching embarrassment---but judging by the sound of Pepe's voice it was nothing good.

Pepe has always been the steadiest man I know. When I heard that worry in his voice I could tell we were in a bad place.

Chokes had told Annie that during the one conversation they had after returning from Mexico.

"It's the sort of place a man will kill you for an egg." Robert grimaced and then looked over at the Cavalier.

"We won't stop," the man in the cape said. "We don't need anything from this town."

Joseph was smiling but only to lighten the mood. They were still close to the border; he probably worried about defections.

"There it is!" Joseph explained as they crested a rise.

"What?" Annie asked; all she saw below them was a field of gravel with a handful of dilapidated, adobe buildings in the distance.

"Los Huesos," Isaac said, his tone of voice was grim

The pueblo was a church, a bar, cemetery, and a handful of flat roofed huts. Everything made by man was crumbling and slowly being reclaimed by the desert. The group rode closer. Dogs that were little more than skeletons with fur came out to sniff at the horses and yap weakly. There was the smell of some beast roasting nearby. A fat man with a heavy looking mustache

114

stumbled out of the church; he was cradling a rifle like a child and glaring at the travelers if they had barged into his home.

"Why did you bring them down here?" He singled out Pepe but spoke English.

Pepe reined his horse and rode over to the man. The conversation switched to Spanish. Annie spoke very little of the language back then and had to ask Pepe sometime later what he and the Mexican had talked about.

I told him that we were looking for the bones of a friend.

"Bones? Why does it matter? If your friend is dead, he does not care."

I tried to explain how El Hombre had saved us and that we were trying to do the honorable thing and bury his bones but that did not make the man with the rifle any less angry.

"There is nothing for them but death down here, more bones to feed to desert. Unless you turn back north I will ride and tell people you are here and they will hunt you."

Annie may not have understood his words but his tone needed no translation. Issac had moved one hand from the reins to his saddlebag where the pistol was waiting, loaded.

I hoped the fat Mexican would try and point his rifle at us and give me an excuse to drill him like I had drilled those trees in Central Park. A few moments later, I felt guilty for wanting such a fate for another human being.

That confession had come a few months later at his Temple in Los Angeles. Just getting those words out had been a struggle and A.R. could see more of them waiting inside as if at a gate. Annie knew the Rabbi enough to know what shape those words left in the dark would take: Why hadn't that dark spark died when he became an older man? Sometimes he thought it was gone but it was insistent, unwilling to die. Before the opportunity came to draw his pistol the Mexican with the rifle said something that was probably a curse and then walked back in the church.

115

"What did he say?" Chokes, shifting uncomfortably in his car seat.

"He doesn't like *norteamericanos,*" The Cavalier smiled reassuringly. "We will come across people like that on our journey, it's nothing to worry about as long as we have a Mexican in our party."

Not waiting for a response, he urged his horse back into a slow walk. Pepe said nothing, torn between his worry and his loyalty to his friends.

Robert put the car back in gear and drove out of Los Huesos with the others. *I could tell Joseph was lying. His tell was a smirk, the same smirk that came across this face when he had been running his schemes in the past. It was nearly enough for me to turn around and head back toward the United States even if I had to make the trip on my own.*

Annie could tell the Cavalier was spinning the truth but she was excited: All those stories about battles between good and evil? Well, odds were good the group would be in the thick of it.

"This place the same as you remember it?" She asked the group in general.

"In some ways: The buildings have fallen down more and the wild dogs are even skinnier," The Cavalier said. "The *feeling* hasn't changed, though---it's an ugly place, A.R., but only a handful of minutes on what will be weeks of adventure."

He laughed at that and sat up proudly in the saddle. A.R. looked back at Robert who was rolling his eyes.

I don't like places that don't change or are in such a backwater that progress can find them, He explained to Annie later. *Why would you live in a world that refuses or is unable to acquire motorcars and electricity and telephones? How could people not embrace all the gifts God and the 20th century had given them? Backwards people disgust me nearly as much as the constant gas Chokes was emitting. Even in that open touring car his flatulence was astounding. It was so thick it seemed you could paint the sky with it.*

116

The Cavalier urged his horse to lead the group. Annie dropped back to see what the men in the touring car were talking about.

"You seem in another world, Mr. Robert."

"Just concerned about our safety, Abel."

"Call me Chokes."

"How did you come about that name?"

"Before I came to work for Mr. Harmon, I worked at a ranch aways north of Los Angeles---"

"I'm from Los Angeles, what city were you near?"

"Nordhoff, just a tiny place. Boss made me responsible for five acres, told me to make it grow. I ain't a gardener but I did as I was told: I got some seeds, planted them, and somehow they did well. Boss wasn't happy, though. All I had planted were five acres of artichokes. So many artichokes we didn't know what to do with them all."

"And that's how you got your name..."

"Yes, sir. It was Artichokes for a while then they shortened it to Chokes."

"Why did you bring the nickname with you down to New Mexico?"

That question threw the cook and he had to think for several moments.

"I've been Chokes so long it'd be strange to be called anything else. Even my wife calls me Chokes."

"Didn't know you're a married man."

"Yessir, thirty-seven years."

"What does she think of you being with us?"

Chokes looked out to his right, maybe at the enormous, four armed saguaro cactus they were passing.

"She knows Senor Pepe is a good man and that I am loyal to him. That's all that matters, I reckon."

"I would reckon she is worried about you," Robert looked over at Chokes meaningfully.

"I would reckon you are probably right."

35
(1957)

"I keep expecting her to pass in the night," Hector said.

Dr. Hernandez was standing next to him as the two doctors checked in on Annie who was asleep.

"It's surprising she still lives after a week," the older doctor said. "Perhaps the internal bleeding is not as bad as we thought."

"Perhaps," Hector agreed with a nod.

But he did not really agree; he believed the patient still lived because she hadn't finished her story.

"How are your brothers' moods this week?" Hector asked Esmerelda a couple of hours later as they checked on Annie.

"Getting better," she smiled. "Maybe they will be willing to talk to you in a couple of days."

"I would like that," the doctor smiled.

The patient stirred, the nurse brought her a cup of water.

"Dr. Hernandez doesn't know I've been talking to you two, does he?" The patient asked weakly.

"You were awake?" Hector asked.

"In a manner of speaking," Annie said after a few sips and then looked over at the darker corner of the room.

"This morning the shadows on the walls became crows," she added.

"Crows?" Esmerelda asked, wondering if the patient made a mistake translating her thoughts into Spanish.

"Si," Annie smiled weakly. "*Cuervos.*"

She sat up a little, grimacing as her guts moved.

"After I saw the crows I was thinking of the men," the patient continued. "How all of them told me stories of when they were young aside from the Cavalier; it was as if he was born fully formed, cape included."

Annie looked over at the corner where she could have sworn there were dark birds.

"On my first trip deep into Mexico I was often at the front of the group. The youngest of an old group, excited and full of energy. It was the same when I returned several years later."

Her recollections made the old woman smile at first but then the smile left her face.

"In the city I had gone a dark way, *down a dark path* as our old priest would say---running to the desert was the best thing I ever did. The harsh light burned away all my nonsense, for a while at least."

Annie looked right in the nurse's face. Esmerelda had never noticed the eyes before, a very faint green as if the desert light had burned away most of the color.

"I could have killed Macho as surely as he has killed me," the patient said softly. "As it turns out, though, I lack the icy grit of all those shootists I read about as a child. Maybe it was because he had been a friend. We saw each other across that courtyard; I hesitated, he did not."

36
(1916)

The group stopped for the night a few miles to the south of Los Huesos in a small barranca. Annie set to making a fire as Chokes went through the provisions to figure out what to make for supper. Joseph watched Robert scowling at the hard ground with what seemed to be amusement.

"Been awhile since you slept rough, I imagine," the Cavalier smiled

"I do not believe I will be sleeping much," Robert scowled.

"How could you not love this--the quiet and the stars that will be out later?"

"I have quiet and stars on my back veranda---and a toilet fifty feet away."

"Chokes brought a shovel for cat holes," the man in the cape gestured towards the cook.

Robert shuddered and kicked at a rock.

"At least I brought toilet paper."

"Toilet paper?" The Cavalier looked surprised.

"You know what toilet paper is, I assume...I *hope*."

"Yes, I just wouldn't have thought to bring any on this trip."

"I don't see any other options around here."

Joseph looked around and frowned.

"You know, you may be right."

"Indoor plumbing and toilet paper will save mankind," Robert nodded.

"What do you mean?"

"Hygiene, washing yourself, keeping clean. Filth has killed more people than wars."

"We'll see what you say when this war is over," Isaac had wandered over to listen in.

"I will say the same; it's a fact," Robert said firmly.

"Maybe---" Isaac said.

"I am grateful to have lived long enough to see how the world has improved. We have flush toilets and electricity, you can even have your appendix taken out if it grows inflamed."

"Appendix?" The Cavalier asked.

"Yes, you remember how I told you my sister died. She would have survived if she had been born thirty years later..."

Robert trailed off. It was nearly dark and both men looked up to study the first visible stars.

"I feel lost in this time," Joseph sighed.

"It's common for aging men, I think," Isaac said solemnly.

"Perhaps, or maybe it's how life has sped up in the past thirty years," The Cavalier gestured towards the Model T. "I don't feel comfortable with all the motorcars and fast pace, it causes me no end of stress."

Robert said nothing. After a minute or so he walked off into the darkness. *Joseph's mewling disgusted me. To me he was a pathetic relic, a stranger in a shabby cape. I couldn't stand to look at him anymore.*

A few minutes later, the wealthy man returned. He rummaged in the back of the Ford until he found a contraption.

"What's that?" Annie asked.

Robert unfolded it a little, it was a wooden toilet seat on folding, metal legs.

"Look at the dude!" The Cavalier laughed.

"My, that is quite the luxurious contraption," Isaac smiled and nodded.

Even Pepe looked amused by the toilet seat on legs. Robert just waved a hand at them before walking off into the dark to do his business. His companions were still chuckling and making comments; each would later, quietly, approach Robert to see if they could borrow the toilet seat on legs.

Annie remembered all of them sitting around the fire that first night. Chokes emerged from the darkness with a bottle of whiskey and Joseph laughed his approval, taking the first drink before passing it to his left. The man on his left was Chokes who looked around at the white faces around the fire---were they *really* okay with a colored man sharing their bottle? As if picking up on his thoughts, the Cavalier smiled and nodded at him and then Isaac did the same.

Gratefully, Chokes took a drink.

"Y'all been friends a long time, right?" The cook asked.

Isaac looked over at the colored man with a shrug.

"Or we were friends a long time ago."

The rabbi paused---had they really been friends? Or, had they simply traveled together? Did he feel close to any of them? He wasn't sure. Pepe looked sad, though, maybe it was because of the *were friends a long time ago* part. Pepe was a good man but overly sensitive.

"And now we are friends again, right?" Isaac gestured at the others around the fire.

"Of course." The Cavalier beamed, he looked at the others in turn but avoided Robert's gaze.

The wealthy man picked up on that and focused on the bottle that had found its way into his hand.

"How did we live like this?" He asked

"Sleeping rough?" Isaac asked.

"Not just that...I guess I am spoiled by modern life."

"It treats some men right, others not so much." Chokes said after taking a small drink.

"I would imagine on the ranch you don't have indoor plumbing, " Robert mused.

"Not for the Mexicans and us Coloreds, but Mr. Harmon does in the main house; had it installed maybe five years back."

"I remember finding scorpions in outhouses," Robert cringed.

"The good old days," Joseph joked. Robert glared at him then stared into the flames.

"I believe I will be turning in. Good night, gentlemen."

The wealthy man rose from the rock he had been sitting on and walked into the darkness where his bedroll lay. Joseph was still smiling but Pepe could tell something was bothering him.

Robert had always been mean, ornery, as Anglos would say. His ways, I think they made him sick, I believe that. He hurt and he lashed out, on our trip he mostly lashed out at Joseph.

Pepe drank deeper than the others but did not seem to get drunk.

"I am worried, Chokes. Maybe it was not a good idea having Sebastian run the ranch."

The cook picked up on Pepe's *real* concerns and smiled warmly at his friend.

"Ah, don't worry none; Mr. Harmon knows he has a good thing with you."

"Perhaps, but I am still a Mexican to him. You know about his grandfather, right?"

"Know he's been dead a long time, that's about it."

"He was killed in the war with Mexico."

"We were in a war with Mexico?" Chokes looked surprised.

"It was before any of us were born," Pepe explained.

"How long before the War Between the States?" The cook asked.

"Maybe twenty years, and the grandfather was killed by the Mexican Army. The Harmons hated Mexicans because of it."

The cook took the bottle from the Cavalier again and looked thoughtful.

"I don't think Mr. Harmon hates Mexicans," he said quietly but firmly. "I never hear him say a bad word about them."

"It's not words, it's a look he has sometimes when a Mexican makes a mess of things."

"I've seen that look, he does it when us colored folk and whites mess things up, too."

"Maybe."

"I can't imagine people hating Mexicans." The Cavalier, as he took the bottle from Isaac. "A fine people, and I'm not just saying that because you're here, Pepe."

The sound of Robert's snores drifted over from the darkness.

"He still has a grudge against you." Isaac, before taking the bottle from Chokes.

"I thought he realized you did not take the silver." Pepe, poking at the fire with a stick.

"It's not about the silver."

"What then?"

Joseph thought for a few moments then shook his head.

"It is a private matter."

"So private you cannot share it in a situation like this?" Isaac frowned.

"A situation like this?"

"Our sacred journey," Isaac gestured out towards the wilderness that surrounded them.

"Is that what this is?" Joseph asked.

"It feels that way." Pepe, took a drink and then passed the bottle to Isaac. The four of them fell into a comfortable silence. The night was still and quiet, even the fire refused to crack. A half moon was somewhere up in the heavens and the bottle was more than half empty.

37
(1957)

"How are you this morning?" Esmerelda asked Annie after pulling a chair up close to the patient's bed.

"Last night my body ached and the sky seemed to be on fire when I looked out the window," the older woman's voice was weak.

This troubled the nurse, she had seen no fire in the sky, but Esmerelda kept her thoughts to herself.

"You have been through a lot, senora."

"You're going to marry that doctor?" Annie smiled. "Ain't ya?"

Before the nurse could answer Hector walked in the room. He made his official inquiries and then dragged a chair close to the bed, right next to Esmerelda's chair and Annie winked at the nurse.

"The pain started off bad last night," the patient said. "So I distracted myself from my own pains by remembering Robert away from his big comfortable house and fancy bed. He probably kept waking up that first night, realized where he was, and had a fit of checking his blankets and clothes for the creatures you find in the desert. What did he dream of? Bones? Friendship? Was he listening to Chokes telling stories? Had they entertained him or were they a drone or a dirge to tune out?"

38
(1916)

One of Annie's most prominent memories of Robert on that trip was how he seemed to be fixated on Joseph's cape. Later, he commented to her about how the sun had faded it before recollecting how the man in the car with him was an overly eager conversationalist.

All that drive, Chokes would talk and talk and talk. I tuned it out to such a degree he practically had to shake me when he interrupted his seemingly endless prattle to ask me something.

"Sorry, the sun---you were asking something?"

"Mr. Harmon calls Mr. Joe *the Cavalier*," the cook said. "How did he get that name?"

"The cape, and the fact that our friend is very cavalier about morality."

Something crossing Abel's face---

Chokes probably thought I was being harsh and showing no loyalty to a friend. He knew nothing.

"It's the cape," Robert clarified. "He looks like he should have been in Europe some time ago flashing a sword around and righting wrongs---that's why they call him the Cavalier."

He smiled at Chokes but the colored man had become solemn.

"You're an angry man, aren't you, Mr. Robert?"

"Am I?"

"Maybe I'm speaking out of turn."

"No, you meant no harm in it, I can see that. I don't know, Chokes..."

"Mr. Joe may be a character, but he seems like a good man under it all."

I remember Chokes saying that and thinking 'It isn't that simple.' I cannot fault him, though, he is a man of a simple nature, either that or he refused to see the darkness in people.

"How did you get to riding with the others? Pepe never told me the story."

"I only rode with them a couple of times. The reason I am even along with the three of them was the situation the four of us four ourselves in."

He recognized that Abel had no idea what he meant and told the story of the day all of them had been saved by the Stoic.

"Looking back it was a good day," Robert concluded with a thoughtful expression. "Nearly being murdered was just a part of the best day of my life. It shook me out of accepting the life my father had scripted for me. He had a store and the plan was for me to eventually take it over. It wasn't just a dry goods store, it was the sort of place that people made a day of riding in to gawp at all the things we sold. By the time I was grown my father was sick, probably with cancer. I took over running the store but he kept a bed in one corner so he could talk to people and make sure the way I kept things was following his vision."

"His vision?"

"I can't explain it, it was more than a store to him. I was good at running it but Daddy was very particular---"

Robert stopped his train of thought. Colored or not, he liked Abel and didn't want Chokes to think less of him; his view of his father was one of little respect as he saw his father as a small man.

"Honestly," Robert continued. "I was sick of the place. Not just the store, the town. Everyone knew me and I knew everyone and that was a problem."

"How was it a problem?"

Robert drove on, seeming to stare at Joseph's back. Abel---normally happily oblivious---was clearly picking up on the fact that he had asked too many questions; things had gotten uncomfortable, *more* uncomfortable. Annie was letting her horse slip back, closer to the car where a serious conversation was taking place. What was Chokes finally picking up on? He wouldn't say when she spoke to him when they were back north.

"They say there's a revolution down here," the cook said, "but it seems peaceful enough."

The tension broke some.

"Hopefully we'll avoid most of it, but that man in Los Huesos seemed set in helping trouble find us." Robert replied.

At least it would be easy to see trouble coming: They were crossing a vast, dry plain that seemed like a hundred miles of dry scrub and rock in every direction.

"Seemed like a bad town," Abel nodded. "Sort of place a man ends up in by mistake."

"No, men always go there on purpose, usually running from something," Robert countered. "We went there after some scheme or other that had gone awry as things with Joseph tend to go awry---things with all of us tended to go awry when we were together. Don't mind me, Chokes, I just have no idea why I'm here."

Chokes left a respectful silence before responding.

"Doing the right thing, I imagine."

"You mean looking for the bones of a man we only came across once?"

"He risked his life to save you---seems a peculiar thing for a stranger to do."

The venom left Robert, he appeared taken by emotions, sadness by the looks of it.

"That was Noah," he said almost too softly for Annie to hear over the engine. "Honorable to the point of it being a character flaw. He was like one of those characters in those novels Isaac read come to life."

"Noah? You mean the fella people call the Stoic?"

"Yes."

"Then you knew him more than the others."

The tension returned. Abel's smile grew meek and then ran for the hills. He probably felt bad for asking something that made Robert uncomfortable but how could he have known? Pepe and Annie talked about Chokes and Robert in that car some weeks later.

I explained to Chokes that Senor Robert is a miserable man, that's all, Pepe told the girl. *A miserable man made sick by his secrets. Chokes was determined not to take it personal and keep telling Robert stories even if they bored the stink out of him.*

Annie's horse was alongside the car; she could see Robert struggling to be decent to his travel companion.

"I apologize if I come across as taciturn, Abel."

"Taciturn?"

"Not an easy man to speak with."

Chokes said nothing. Robert realized they had fallen behind and sped up some.

"Sometimes I wish I had ridden with the others more back then because I have no idea what I missed; in reality it was probably a good thing to miss."

"Sounds like an adventure from what Pepe told me."

"He speaks a lot about his days riding with Robert and Issac?"

"We get on well, drink sometimes together, not that our women like it. The two of us are just old men with our stories."

"What about you, Abel? You seem to have gotten around some."

"I reckon so, came from back east like Mr. Isaac."

"Back east, you mean the South?"

Abel got a strange look on his face.

"You think us plantation folk?" He looked over at Robert and smiled, but it was not his usual gentle smile.

"I meant no offense, Abel."

"I know, and I took none. There's a reason why I'm like this."

"Like what?"

"We all play roles, don't we?" Abel nodded towards the Cavalier. "Some of us have to tell lies in order to survive."

It seemed another man had slipped into Abel's skin or maybe he had just been hiding there, waiting for the right time to step from behind the disguise. *We all play roles, don't we? Some of us have to tell lies in order to survive.*

Robert knew that was true, he understood that more than most men; Chokes had probably seen that.

"My Daddy was educated for a colored man. He ran north when he was young---"

"He was a part of the Underground Railroad?"

"I guess. He got up to New England and a white family took him in. Daddy couldn't read or write but he took to it well. He could have had a good life up there, but he wasn't at peace."

Chokes looked out in the distance, when he continued his voice was soft.

"Foolish things he did when he had a family at home. Daddy wouldn't give up, though. I did, he couldn't. I think all those years in New England he had been planning what he did."

"What do you mean you gave up and he couldn't?"

Abel seemed to ignore the question.

"He went back home, back down south, to make things right. Momma told him the War would sort things out, that most folks like the people who had owned Daddy would be killed or punished in some way, but Daddy didn't listen. He went back down to Arkansas in '64 and we never saw him again."

"You don't know what happened to him?"

"No. I looked for him some years after the War, even went back to the place he had run from. None of the colored folks had seen him, maybe he died even before he got there."

Abel was rubbing one hand on the dashboard as if he were polishing it.

131

"I was like him for a while," the cook continued, his voice deeper than usual, "but it wore away. I was like my daddy and it brought trouble; unlike him, I could walk away when things got rough; guess that makes me weak."

"No." Or did Robert say that because of his own way of running from things?

Chokes stopped rubbing the dashboard and looked out at the dead land they were driving through.

"Now we're in the middle of another war---"

"At least we aren't fighting it."

"Not now, but I'd bet cash money we will. Things I read about that war...it's like a monster that's gonna just get bigger and bigger until it eats up the world."

"No, someone will give up before then."

Did Robert really believe that?

I was horrified by what was happening in Europe even as I was making money off it.

"Maybe." Abel was smiling or trying to: They had been riding too long in darkness and it seemed to Annie that the cook felt the need to break it.

"Ain't we a hoot, Mr. Robert? Five very different fellas and A.R. over there traveling together."

The *Happy Colored Fellow* disguise was back in place. Robert said nothing. They had an understanding: Two men keeping secrets from the world.

39
(1916)

Pepe kept thinking about the angry man back in Los Huesos---

I will tell people about you and they will hunt you.

He kept seeing the man, how he had cradled his rifle like a baby, and understood that it had not been an empty threat. It didn't matter if Pepe was Mexican, he would have been gunned down with the others.

I was worried that it would be worse for me, that they would see me as a traitor,

He was riding beside Isaac in the middle of the pack. Behind them, the car was chugging along as they left the plains for an area with many washes, Chokes and Robert talking.

"You look troubled."

Isaac: He had gotten his horse so close it was nearly brushing Pepe's leg.

"Troubled?" Pepe asked.

"Like you have a lot on your mind."

"This is a bad idea. We need to do this, pay our debt, but it is still a bad idea."

"You're a good man, Pepe. You have no need to be here, so you're probably the best of the four of us."

"I don't know, El Hombre saved me, as well."

"He was saving Robert, we were just Robert's friends."

"Then why are you here?"

Isaac thought of the gun in his saddlebag; it made him smile, he couldn't help it.

"I never really changed, I just got older."

It took Pepe a few seconds but he finally understood, remembering how calm and deadly the Jew had been during the ambush.

"I don't think any of us changed," Pepe said softly. "The world just changed around us."

The rabbi looked over at the ranch manager with a softness he infrequently revealed to his traveling companions.

"I envy you, I always have. You have a good heart, how does a man not lose a good heart in this world?"

Pepe said nothing in response for a few seconds.

"I don't know how good I am..."

"Okay, well, maybe compared to us." Isaac shrugged in the direction of the car.

Pepe understood how the others saw him. There had never been much space in their conversations---(Joseph's monologues, Isaac's terse responses, and Robert's interjections)---for Pepe's own words. He had learned to settle for nodding and smiling and occasionally chuckling.

What you said about it being a role, my place in our friendship...it is a good way to describe it. When we were no longer around each other I moved on and became my own man, a leader, someone in charge. When we got back together it was difficult for me to find my place again. There was something else, another reason it had been good for me when I stopped riding with Joseph.

"I wish Robert would stop thinking that Joseph took the silver," Pepe said with a frown. "I think he has gotten you believing that as well but I can tell you that Joseph did not take it."

Isaac just looked over at him.

I could see that Isaac understood what I was hinting at. I did not know what to feel---relief? Fear he would tell the others? Probably both things.

"I'm sure you had your reasons," Isaac sighed.

There it was after thirty years: *I'm sure you had your reasons.*

"I did. Things to do with my family, that's all I can say."

"You could have told me, could have told Joseph, too."

"I could not because I cannot pay it back. The silver is gone."

"How did you even manage to get it without us knowing?"

134

"Because the two of you would never suspect me," Pepe replied. "Neither of you ever saw any grit in me, that I could do such a thing."

He looked around for eavesdroppers, somehow missing Annie.

"You know what makes it really bad?" Pepe continued. "I felt no guilt. I always thought I saw you as my friends, but I never felt bad for what I did."

"But you looked hurt when I said that we *used* to be friends."

"I *felt* hurt, but I slept well last night. I thought about what you said. At first it hurt, but then I looked back at the way things really were---not the stories I have told Chokes about the good times."

Pepe struggled for words; none that came to mind seemed to fit.

"I want to be the man you three have always seen me as, simple and kind, the good one---"

"You are, but not simple---"

"No. You know nothing about me because I was the only one listening. Joseph was always talking or the two of you were arguing with him or each other."

Emotions were overwhelming the Mexican so he stopped talking. Isaac left room for a respectful silence before responding.

"I'm sorry, Pepe."

His companion looked over at him with bitterness, it looked odd on his normally gentle face.

"Why would you be sorry? I took the silver. I cannot be the man you used to see as your friend---if any of us were ever friends."

The sound of the engine was getting fainter, Robert and Chokes were falling behind as the rocks got larger and harder to get around. Isaac and Pepe called out to Joseph to stop. The man with the cape rode back and the three of them stood together to watch Robert maneuver the car around the rocks gingerly. The back wheels spun when the Model T dipped into a wash and became mired in deep gravel.

"This is Hell." Pepe, so softly the others barely heard.

"No, I don't believe Hell is quite this inhospitable." The Cavalier, with a wry smile.

"I took the silver." Pepe looked at him, surprising himself with the viciousness with which the words came out.

The three men looked at each other. In the distance, Robert was yelling an obscenity.

"I know." Joseph's smile had become almost angelic.

"What do you mean, *I know*?" Isaac, loud enough that the men in the car had forgotten their own troubles and had looked over.

"I knew he had a good reason for taking it," Joseph said softly.

"And you assume that my reasons were honorable..."

Pepe was smiling a terrible smile as he stared in the distance and shook his head. Maybe they *were* in Hell, how otherwise could the change to their friend be explained?

Maybe we all died years ago, maybe we died in the shootout and only thought the Stoic saved us.

"I'm not going to let this nonsense get me down," Joseph whispered.

"What?"

"Nevermind. I am sorry if you feel that we wronged you, Pepe."

"Wronged *me*? I took the silver, Joseph."

"It was just money. Look at me, do I look like money means anything to me? I know the three of you look down on me, how shabby my life is while the three of you have gone on to success."

"Hey, a little help over here!" Robert called out.

Ignoring the man in the car, Joseph reined in his horse so he could focus on Pepe.

"You think I always looked at you as the simple, kind man; the good-hearted Mexican. No, I could never be friends with a truly decent man. Decent men make me ill at ease."

Pepe had no response. Isaac was rubbing his saddle bag and looking up at the sky.

"We're not going to tell Robert about the silver," he said.

Joseph nodded at him and then turned his attention to Pepe, getting close enough so that he could keep his voice low.

"You are good, Pepe. Honestly, we are all good---I want to believe that."

"I needed to tell you, all three of you---"

"Let his hate be directed at me and me only."

"You said it wasn't just about the silver, you said there was something else."

"There is."

"And you won't tell us---*here? Now?*"

"The two of you already know his secret. We may never speak of it, but all three of us know."

The three of them just looked at each other. Annie felt left out but knew it was not her place to ask about Robert's secret.

"We'd best get that car out of the wash," Isaac motioned over towards the Ford.

All four riders started heading towards the Model T.

"We need to find a good route through this area," Pepe took in their surroundings. "If we keep going straight there are many washes."

"We may need to backtrack a few miles," Joseph said.

"I can ride off towards that escarpment, maybe from the top I can see a way around it," Pepe offered.

"Do you think you'll be back by dark?" Isaac looked doubtful.

"Maybe, but there is a full moon so it won't be bad."

"We'll set up camp here. God, if only there was shade."

Pepe shook his canteen. Joseph picked up on the fact it sounded half empty and handed his over. The two men looked at each other.

"You are my friend, Joseph."

"As you are mine, and Isaac's."

"Eh, the two of you are alright, I guess." The rabbi shrugged before smiling.

"We'll see you by morning?" He asked.

"Yes."

Pepe rode off and the other men on horseback watched him grow smaller, shimmering like a mirage in the heat.

40
(1916)

The next morning Pepe came across a road a couple miles west of the rocks that had stopped the car. It was little more than two wheel tracks.

"You sure you don't want to ride in the car, Pepe? You must be tired."

"No." Pepe smiled faintly, he was tired but he didn't want to sleep.

I was relieved after telling Joseph and Isaac what I had done. I felt like I actually was a good man, not a liar, not someone who keeps important things from his friends. When I rode to the top of the escarpment, however, my mind went to bad places. All of you looked so small, so insignificant...and I thought I could make out the ranch up north---how far was it? Forty miles? I just stared at all of you, unable to see your faces or hear your voices, you may as well have been ants. What if I had rode back to the ranch and left you there? In my heart I knew that there was nothing but death out there, that under your skin there were more bones to feed the desert.

The man in Los Huesos hadn't been lying; Pepe had heard lots of stories from the other Mexicans at the ranch. Stories they did not tell the norteamericanos. The six of them were in a land of trouble. Some called Pancho Villa a hero and others argued that his men did terrible things in his name. Pepe had stood up on that escarpment looking in all directions but mostly north---home. He no longer considered himself Mexican; he was proud of the people he had come from, but he no longer felt Mexican.

I seriously considered riding back to the ranch. I was not ready to die, my life was too good to abandon.

But in the end he had ridden back to where his companions were camped, to men who may or may not have been his friends. He couldn't leave them and realizing that felt good, like maybe he had actually become a better man than he had been in the past.

Pepe was nodding off on his horse when the four of them met up with an ancient man on a burro led by his grandson. Neither spoke English and their accents were heavy enough that Joseph couldn't converse with them in Spanish. The young man seemed angry at the presence of *los gringos*.
If they meet up with any of Villa's men, he will definitely tell them about us.
His grandfather was trying to calm him, but the younger man kept brushing off his elder, going so far as to call him a fool in front of the strangers.
"You want me to be polite, *abuelo*? Men like this have been the ruin of our country."
"Eh, su quarell debe estar con los gobiernos, no hombres."
"What is that old fellow saying?" Isaac asked.
"He is telling his grandson that we are not the problem, our country is," Pepe explained.
"That's good---"
"Yes, except the grandson isn't buying it."
The old man was looking right at Joseph. His skin looked like leather but his eyes were bright, almost golden, and locked with Joseph's. With much difficulty, he climbed off the burro and walked to where the man with the cape was sitting on his horse. Joseph climbed down out of respect. The old man started talking with Pepe translating between the two men.
"The boy does not know history," the old *Mexicano* said. "He does not understand that borders do not matter, if anything they cause problems. You all are men, I am a man. Yes?"
"Yes, indeed." The Cavalier smiled.

"You look old enough to remember the way things were, before *that*," the older man gestured towards the Model T with a scowl. "*El carruaje de satanás.*"

"I take it he doesn't like cars," Robert said with little interest.

"He called it the devil's carriage," Pepe was smirking.

"He can tell it to his piles," Robert replied. "They must be the size of a fist after riding that burro."

"There is a white man in these parts," the old man continued. "A bad man wearing the face of a good man. He says he is a pastor, but he is of the Devil if anything."

"Is he riding alone?" Joseph asked.

"Yes."

"What kind of a fool would ride alone in Mexico in these times?" Isaac frowned.

"A man who does not feel fear about other men," the old man shook his head.

"And he is looking for you." The grandson said that with a horrible smile.

"Us? No one knows we are here but the people Pepe works for."

"He knows you are in Mexico," the boy nodded. "He said there would be a man in a cape, a Jew, a rich man--"he turned to Pepe with contempt. "And *un traidor de un Mexicano.*"

"The Holy Man," Joseph said softly. "I did not know he still lived."

"Who is this *holy man*?" Isaac, looking at Joseph as if he had been holding a secret.

"He worked for Joseph Starn back in the old days," the Cavalier explained.

"A shootist?" Isaac asked.

"Not really. More like Starn's Pinkerton man, can find anyone anywhere."

"Why would he be after us?" Isaac demanded.

And then he understood as did Joseph and they both looked at Pepe.

"What are you two talking about?" Robert, who had not been told about Pepe stealing the silver.

"The Holy Man is tracking us, he works for Jason Starn," Joseph explained.

"Why? We didn't take his silver, after all." He shot Joseph a meaningful look.

"Maybe Starn is angry with one of our group about more than the silver," Joseph said harshly.

The other three friends were surprised, never having heard Joseph yell or even speak with anger. Joseph shook his head and turned back to the old man.

"We are looking to find the bones of a friend of ours. They were found by Apaches maybe thirty or forty miles to the south and east of here."

"Apache? There are very few of them left," the old man averted his eyes, Annie could tell he was hiding something.

"Do you know where we can find them--and not get killed?" Isaac asked.

"That last part...*Se pide algo que puede ser imposible.* But, if you follow this road to Hermosa Delante, you may find an Apache."

"Muchas gracias."

The old man waved off Joseph's thanks and turned to his grandson.

"*Ayúdame copia de seguridad chico rudo.*"

The boy gingerly helped his grandfather back onto the burro.

"You are welcome in my land," the old man smiled. "But I am just one man, you know? Maybe it would be best to go home, yes?"

"We owe a great debt, senor. We have to do this."

"Ah, yes, I can see that. *Buen viaje y que Dios los vea el hogar.*"

"What did he say now?" Robert, still stinging from Joseph's anger.

"Safe travels and may God see you home."

41

(1957)

Esmerelda set up a privacy curtain around Annie's bed and cleaned the older woman up. Removing the bandages, the wounds appeared to be healing but there was still the smell of bowel. You could not see any signs of internal bleeding, but the woman seemed weak and pale and there was blood in her stool. The nurse understood her face must have betrayed her concerns. because the patient smiled kindly and put a hand on the nurse's arm.

"This is not the first time I have ridden into the arms of death," Annie said.

"What do you mean? Are you talking about when you rode down to Mexico with your friends?"

The patient's hand dropped to her side and she winced when Esmerelda replaced the bandages.

"I am not speaking of the journey the six of us made during the Revolution," the older woman said. " I understood even then we were not really in danger. No, I am speaking of when I returned alone, still young enough to believe I could do what I pleased and everything would work out. The Revolution was over, things were quiet and I was young and strong and acquainted with roughing it."

Annie stopped, she was very weak; feeble and yet determined to finish her story.

"Maybe I am at peace because it is my time or maybe it is because I still feel that God will rescue me in the end: My insides will heal and I will leave this hospital on my own feet and not in a box."

She paused, her face dark as the shadows in the corner of the room.

"No," Annie continued in such a soft voice the nurse had to learn forward to hear what she was saying. "I understood from the moment that shot rang out in the courtyard distinct from all those shots being fired that I had been murdered."

Hector walked in, Esmerelda knew his footsteps.

"*Un momento,*" the nurse said. "I am dressing our patient."

Annie could feel Hector smiling even if she couldn't hear him, she told the doctor that later: *I have enjoyed this, watching you two fall in love.*

He had protested, but the older woman just smiled and laughed weakly. *Trust an older woman, doctor.*

"The second time I went to Mexico things went bad after three days," Annie said after the curtain had been put away. "I had too little water---it's always those easy mistakes that kill you. The end seemed close and then I saw a vast sea of pink shimmering in the distance; Hermosa Delante. The town where every building had been painted pink when I had been there last and apparently still was. It was in Hermosa Delante that I became friends with Macho. It took him awhile to deduce that I was a woman and by then our relationship was already firm and my sex was not an issue. He found it strange I was carrying a pistol and warned me against it."

The patient shrugged towards the water and Esmerelda got her a glass.

"I imagine many people would not take kindly to a *gringa* with a gun so soon after the Revolution," Hector opined.

"I pretended to listen as people who believe they know everything do," Annie continued. "All those books I had read about the old days were still haunting me, maybe they still do. Macho warning me off guns is kind of funny now; maybe *ironico* is the right word seeing as he would be the one who gunned me down."

The patient stopped, looked off towards the window. When she spoke again her tone was deeper, huskier.

"Our relationship changed in those seconds. I could see his firmness when he pulled the trigger change to remorse when I staggered off; he was still my friend, but even if I had survived that friendship would not be the same. It was the same when Pepe confessed about taking the silver. He murdered something, maybe his role in their group. It left all of them confused: The Cavalier was supposed to be the shifty fellow and Pepe the decent one. If that wasn't the case, where did they all stand after thirty years?

42
(1916)

Isaac looked over at the old man on the burro receding behind them, wondering his story, fascinated by the possibilities. The man had to be a hundred if he was a day. He had probably seen the French come and go, revolutions---or maybe he had been a simple *peon* isolated from the rest of the country on a small rancho. Pepe probably hadn't translated everything the old man had said. He had probably left out things just as he had left out the *small detail* of stealing Jason Starn's silver.

And now someone is tracking us, Isaac thought, *to what end? He probably thinks we buried it down here, just salted it away in a hole like we're pirates or something.*

The Rabbi looked twenty feet away at Joseph's cape fluttering as he rode, imagining all of them wearing swords and feathered hats.

Pirates, maybe that was all we were; all we needed was scurvy and a couple of parrots.

"Robert tells me that you're a rabbi." Chokes, leaning out the Model T as it got close to Isaac.

"Yes, I have a temple back in Los Angeles."

"So...you're a religious man?"

"I suppose. I have a gun in my saddlebag, though, so I guess it depends on what you consider a religious man."

"Robert tells me that you protected your friends just as a man of God protects his people."

That clearly pleased Isaac, though he tried to cover it up.

"I hadn't looked at it that way," the rabbi said.

Chokes sat back in his seat, choosing his words carefully.

"Back in the day, did you ever lose your religion?"

"What do you mean?"

"When you were carrying a gun and making money however you made money back in the day."

"No…it was always here. I'd see it in people, in trees, in amazing, wild places like this. God is everywhere, I see Him in everything."

"Did you worry that the way you were living would anger Him?"

"Yes, but I knew that He knew my heart, that I would make things right down the road."

That seemed to please Chokes. The automobile was making his horse uneasy so Isaac rode ahead.

Isaac urged his horse on and rode past Joseph.

"I am going aways ahead; I'll wait up for you down the road."

The slow pace of the horses was making him impatient---why hadn't *all* of them taken a truck or something? The trip would have been over in days instead of weeks. The rabbi had grown accustomed to the fast pace of Los Angeles with its automobiles and the general rush to get further into the twentieth century. Young people in his temple told him about moving pictures like the Mack Sennet comedies. There was one comedian, Charlie Chaplin, that a few people had told him was amazing. Isaac was curious but worried how being seen at a moving picture would affect his reputation. He resented it, being denied something as innocent as seeing a movie, but what could he do? Even before Joseph had arrived the rabbi had been thinking of when he had been *free*, those months between leaving his family in New York and returning to his studies in Los Angeles: Sleeping out in the open. Doing whatever he pleased. Carrying a gun. Why had he stopped? Maybe it was because of what he had told Abel:

He knew my heart, that I would make things right down the road.

"You look fit to be tied."

Joseph had made a point to reach Isaac before the others did.

"I don't know why we're on horseback, it seems like we're dragging this out."

"Have you been seduced by the mad rush pace of the modern world, too?"

"You can stay out here and have your adventures, I have to go back to the real world at some point---all three of us do."

"And you see me as cavorting in some imaginary land or something?"

"I wouldn't say *cavorting*, your cavorting days are behind you, my friend."

"What is bothering you so much, Isaac?"

"I miss this and *that* bothers me. I know I don't want to live like this anymore, I am too old and tired to think on my feet, but I miss not having to answer to anyone."

"But you're a rabbi, you are the head of your temple---"

"The rabbi has people to answer to, people and others." He looked up at the sky meaningfully.

"If God put a love of this life in your heart, then didn't He mean for you to pursue it?"

"No. He puts things like that there to test you. Look, I can't even talk about this; tell me about the Holy Man."

"We need to ride on so we can speak privately. You're welcome to join us, A.R."

They rode on for a minute or so and then Isaac looked over at Joseph expectantly.

"What is so secret that you can't tell the others?"

"I feel the need to speak with you at first, to get your counsel."

"Okay."

"You know my people are from Kansas, right?" Joseph asked.

"Yes."

"My father supported the Southern cause. He didn't join the fight because he had to run the farm, but he made many friends that were associates of Robert Lee. After the War, they headed west and many of them crossed our farm. My father would give them sanctuary, fresh horses, whatever they needed. I believe the Holy Man was one of them. After running into that old man on the burro, I got to thinking about the Holy Man, how I had seen him in the company of Jason Starn back in Deming---and then older memories came back."

"So, he is very old, maybe a decade older than you---early seventies, maybe?"

"The thing is, when I remember him on our farm, he looks pretty much the same as he did in Deming fifteen years later."

"How is that so strange? Maybe he was around thirty after the War and 45 when you saw him in New Mexico."

"I can't explain it, the way he was, you'd have to experience it."

"Considering how much trouble he can make for us, I hope I do not."

An hour later, the track cut through a narrow gorge in an immense rock formation. On the other side was the pueblo of Hermosa Delante. Every building was colored pink, even the cantinas. Two men on horseback, both wearing white, came out to greet them. Both men were heavily armed but friendly, calling out to the Cavalier in English.

"Do you have weapons with you?"

"No. We do not."

"Very good; we do not allow guns in Hermosa Delante."

Isaac thought of what was in his saddlebag and wondered how they would be punished for lying.

We are old men, that is probably how they see us, not threats.

And then he thought about how many years had passed since he had shot his pistol.

Maybe they are right.

"Do you mind if we ask your business here?" The other local asked.

"We have heard that a friend of ours died in the desert to the south. We are here to find his bones and take them home for burial."

The one who had been speaking looked doubtful.

"This is a big desert; it hides the bones of many men."

"And there are a lot of people down here who do not like men from the north like you." His companion added with a rueful nod.

"We are looking for an Apache," Isaac had ridden up beside Joseph. "An old man told us we could find an Apache in your town."

The locals were acting confused but the Cavalier could see through it or so he told Annie when they camped for the night.

"I am sorry you came all this way for nothing; all the Apache are dead," the local who had just spoken added.

Oh? Even though I could tell by his face that he was part Apache himself.

"Please." Joseph's voice was gentle. He made himself calm and kindly, just an old traveler and nothing more. "We mean him or her no harm."

"Then why did you lie about having weapons?" The vaguely Apache one was nodding at Isaac.

"We are scared that you would confiscate them; my friends and I know that *gringos* are not welcome in Mexico."

The part Apache stared at Isaac, clearly recognizing something in his face.

"*Usted usa la ropa de un hombre santo, pero usted es claramente un asesino. Un asesino de edad, pero sigue siendo un asesino.*"

"I'm sorry, I do not speak Spanish," Isaac said, annoyed.

"He said that despite your clothes you are a dangerous man."

"I mean no harm to this Apache, I swear to my God---"

"Even though he may have killed the man you seek?"

"Our friend is dead. He was a shootist, it was expected he would meet a violent end."

"As he did."

Townspeople had begun to surround the travelers. None of them appeared welcoming. Counting the locals, Isaac realized that two pistols and a rifle were meaningless against their numbers.

"You know about the man whose bones we seek?" The rabbi asked.

"Yes. He was ambushed maybe thirty miles south and east of here, up in the mountains some. It wasn't Apaches, though, it was Mormons."

"Mormons? I thought they were chased out of here a few years ago."

"Your friend was killed several years ago. This Apache you seek, he could not carry the body out as he was on foot. He took a gun belt and boots as your friend clearly did not need them."

"Why would a Mormon gun our friend down?"

The Mexicans looked at each other and then turned back to Isaac.

"We do not know, *senor*." They appeared to be telling the truth.

"*Usted Gringos debe seguir adelante!*" An old woman in the crowd who had to be at least ninety.

"*Vamos a estar fuera por la caída de la noche. Sin embargo, tenemos que encontrar a alguien,*" The Cavalier smiled with a wave of his hat.

"What did you tell them?"

"I told them that all Jews are the devil and we have delivered you into their arms."

"Joseph---"

"I promised we'd leave their curiously pink town once we spoke to this Apache."

The crowd was parting and a man---clearly a full blood Apache---made his way to where the gringos were. He was anywhere between forty and sixty, tall and proud looking. When he spoke, his English was flawless and unaccented.

"I am the one who found your friend. I believe he was known as the Stoic up north."

"Yes. I am Joseph and this is Isaac and A.R. Back in the motorcar are Abel and Robert, over there is Pepe."

"I know your names."

"You do?"

"Yes. The Holy Man has been looking for you."

"You know of the Holy Man?"

The man's face betrayed nothing, but there was a brief glint of something in his eyes: Fear.

"Yes."

"And what is your name?" the Cavalier asked.

"I will not trouble you with my real name. You can find one amongst yourself if it suits you, I will even answer to it."

"Can you help us find the bones of our friend?"

"Yes."

A woman, probably half blood had walked up beside the Apache,

"We need money. Ask them for money." She said this in Spanish.

The Apache, having heard Joseph speak Spanish, smiled at him.

"*Senora*, it is not only the Mexican over there that speaks as they do in this town."

"You are correct. When she says *we----*"

"Do not listen to her," the Apache said curtly, his smile vanishing as quickly as it had appeared. "I am the last Apache, the very last one."

"We can pay you a fair price for your services as a guide."

"Would ten dollars do the trick?" Isaac asked.

"Dollars are meaningless here, I need pesos."

"How about two hundred pesos?" Joseph asked before looking at his friends.

"We do have enough pesos right?"

"I believe so," Robert sighed.

"I will do it for three hundred, but if we see Villa's men I will leave you."

"Very well."

Isaac kept looking at the woman:

We need money--there are more of them. Maybe they're half breeds like her, maybe he is the last full blood, but I doubt it.

"I will meet you on the other end of town in an hour. I need to saddle my horse and grab my provisions."

"Maybe we could meet you in one of the cantinas."

The Apache smiled ruefully.

"You are not welcome here. We are roughly five heartbeats away from the town sweeping in on you with stones and knives."

"Why is that?"

"Veracruz." Isaac said softly. "That would be the first of many guesses I have."

"Yes. Now, please, ride through before the good Lord denies me my three hundred pesos. I will meet you where you can no longer see the town in exactly one hour."

That said, he vanished back into the crowd.

"Harold." The Cavalier, shaking the reins to get his horse moving.

"What?" Isaac, forcing his own horse into motion.

"We will call him Harold the Apache."

"Is he really a *Harold*?"

"You got a better name?"

Isaac looked out at the open desert; there was just miles of no towns and people that clearly wouldn't help them if they were in trouble.

"No."

43
(1916)

After precisely an hour, Harold the Apache appeared again and the group set off.

"It is an honor to come across an Apache after so many years." The Cavalier said, urging his horse on so he could ride next to their guide.

Harold didn't even look over at him.

"We will be leaving the road soon, that car may not make it," he said tonelessly.

"Robert will not ride on a horse."

"Then Robert probably has no business traveling in a place like this."

The Cavalier started to object but then realized the Apache was probably right.

I could see that there is no point in attempting to befriend this man: We are nothing more to him than wallets with legs and words that spill from them--- too many words.

The road broke into two factions. Off to the left was what appeared to be a footpath. Harold looked from it to the automobile and then back at the trail.

"We can continue on the road. It will cost us maybe ten miles but there is another road that will get us close to your friend."

The Apache continued down the road without another word, not bothering to see if the strangers were following.

"Not the nicest fellow in the world," Isaac, uncapping his canteen.

"Look at what we did to the Apache. Can you blame him?" the Cavalier said. "He probably came down here to get away from us and we just popped up like evil genies."

The rabbi shook the canteen at him and Joseph took it.

"This is a very uncomfortable situation. We have no friends down here, Joseph, no one who will stand up for us. We're too old to be this alone."

"Speak for yourself." Joseph, handing back the canteen with a nod of thanks.

Robert watched Isaac and Joseph passing the canteen back and forth as they spoke.

Old friends, an old married couple, almost. That was the way it had been back in the day as well. Pepe must have felt like a third wheel much of the time.

"Imagine, a real live Apache; can't wait to tell the boys back at the ranch." Chokes. He had been going on about how to make the perfect biscuit and had somehow diverted his monologue to include their sullen guide.

"They won't believe you, I'd imagine."

"Probably not."

"Nor would any of my friends back home," Robert added.

Were the people Robert spent time with really his *friends*? They did business, went hunting, and drank together, but were they *really* friends?

One reason I love the city is that there is so much going on and I have so many responsibilities that there is no time to think earnestly and deeply. Out there in the wilderness, there was nothing to do but think earnestly and deeply. Lord knows my mind drifted to escape Chokes' endless prattle. I thought about the men I referred to my friends and how I felt no attachment to them. The truth was that they didn't know me. In fact, I have always felt obliged to keep a lot of myself secret from them. With such an obligation between us, how could they be my friends?

"You've got indoor plumbing, I'd imagine," Abel said.

"Two water closets." Did it sound like he was boasting? He hadn't meant it that way.

"*Two*? I'll be."

"How did we live without them? How did we just squat over holes in the ground?" He looked around at the miles of rocks surrounding them. "How did we live without automobiles or electricity?"

"We just did. We had no choice and we didn't know no better." Chokes looked down at the dashboard, finding the right words. "I don't know about these times. Maybe we have cars and electricity and moving pictures, but we also have that war in Europe---men just slaughtering each other like it was nothing."

"Happened in the Civil War, too."

"I don't know, no disrespect but I'm not sure if I agree, Mr. Robert."

"How do you see it?"

"I don't know. All I can say is that what I've seen of this century is ugly." They rode on in silence for a minute or so. The car backfired and Annie's horse shied. Robert looked over at her apologetically before addressing Chokes.

"I've lost track of the number of times I've almost turned back on this trip."

"What stopped you?"

"It's not right, leaving a man to the jackals; even if he's only bones."

"Especially if he was a good friend." Chokes nodded.

Robert looked over at the colored man carefully, studied his face, and turned back to the road when he understood that he was still safe, *unseen*.

"Yes," he agreed softly. "Especially then."

A figure was waiting up ahead on horseback. Chokes rested a hand on the rifle leaning against the seat. That night when they made camp he told Annie what had been going through his head. Though sunlight was hitting it the gun felt cold, a reminder of the death it could create. That thought made the whole situation real for the cook and he felt scared. Could he point that rifle at another man? He had been in dire situations before and hadn't liked the results when he had to point a gun at another man and then fire it; seeing the fellow jerk as the bullet changed him forever, seeing the pain turning his face into a small, tortured thing---hearing him beg and moan and finally make no more sounds. Chokes took his hand off the rifle and put his hands in his lap.

"Guns are meaningless." The Apache said that as the Cavalier and Annie caught up to him.
"Why did you have to say that?"Joseph muttered.
"I read a story once, a doctor that creates people from the parts of the dead---"
"Frankenstein?" Annie asked.
Harold looked back at her with a smile equally cold and pleased.
"Meeting the Holy Man reminds me of that story."
"You can read English, I take it."
The Apache looked over at Joseph, then faced forward and subtly rolled his eyes as he shook his head.

A few minutes down the road, they came upon a rider approaching them. He was all in white, even his sombrero, and smiling like a happy fellow.
"You found a guide, I see." The man on horseback was grinning but waves of cold were coming off him despite the heat of the day, both Annie and the Cavalier felt it.
"Yes," Joseph found a smile somehow. "Word has it that you're on our trail."
"Mr. Starn is looking for something he misplaced around thirty years ago."
The Cavalier was now close enough to see that the Holy Man looked exactly the same as he had back in Deming in the 80's and right after the War. How?
I do not want to know the answer to that, I really don't.
His horse and the one the Apache rode were restless, making protests and stirring the earth with their hooves as if writing out the tension they felt.
"Mr. Starn should know we do not have what he seeks."

The Holy Man looked at Joseph and then through him.

"Maybe *you* do not, Joseph Seller, but *one* of you knows."

He focused on Pepe who had approached the group and then shook his head with a chuckle.

"Such a noble quest, riding down here into danger to find the bones of the man who saved you so long ago."

He reined in his horse and rode through the party, stopping to look at each of our faces.

"Tell me then, how are such men lacking nobility on such a quest? How is Mr. Starn to believe that men such as yourselves could be so altruistic?"

He was now behind them, seeming to look down the road they were about to travel. Not just the horses felt something powerful and strange and dark.

"I will leave you gentlemen to whatever finds you down here."

The Holy Man touched the brim of his hat and rode on.

44
(1957)

"I have seen him again. It is a dream. It is not a dream."
Annie said that in a tone of voice neither Hector nor Esmerelda had heard before; it sounded like another person, maybe a ghost, both of them got goosebumps.

"Isaac wrote that in a letter," the patient continued. "It was an old letter by the time I got it. Half had been made unreadable by water: *I have seen him again. It is a dream. It is not a dream."*

She stopped and looked in the part of the room where the crows had been.

"There was no confusion as to who Isaac meant, it was clearly the Holy Man. The first time I saw him was in Mexico. No, seeing him in Mexico reminded me of when I had seen him before. The boarding house. I had been sick enough that my mother thought I was going to die. The fever lasted---days? Weeks? Hours? A strange man came into my room. He was kind, seemed to be checking on me. Came to my room more than once. Always dressed in white, head to toe. When the fever broke I asked my mother about the 'boarder who had checked on me.' She was upset and the shards of her upset cutting into me woke me up fully---of course she was upset, a strange man had been in my room when I was helpless. Mother asked what the man looked like. I described him and she looked relieved.

It must have been your fever; there is no one who looks like that here."
Annie fainted. She was out for a couple of hours. When Hector checked on her the patient was so still the doctor wondered if she had passed. He got close to check for a pulse Annie grabbed his wrist and he cried out.

"Siento, doctor."

"It's okay, I thought---"

159

He didn't want to say it, luckily the patient seemed to understand what he was thinking.

"I replay the scene in the courtyard more than is healthy--the moment when my dying began in earnest. When it was playing out I was too focused on the men I faced who were armed. Now, past the worry of being shot, I can look out to the surrounding areas---the truck and car Don Hector's men came in. A figure is standing between them smiling with the sort of benevolence only the Devil can possess. You know who I speak of."

He understood; understood that she was a dying woman seeing things, ghosts, a man who would be well over a hundred years old. Impossible. *Are you so sure?*

45
(1916)

Robert had seen the Holy Man focus on Pepe before riding off; he got every bit of subtext the ominous stranger was slipping under their door.

Pepe. One of us did take the silver but it wasn't Joseph.

But, what did he do with that information even if his perception was correct? *Of the four of us, Pepe is the most true, the kindest: If he took that silver then there was a good reason, his family probably needed it.*

But still, Pepe had lied...Pepe had ignored his chance to confess when Robert had been accusing Joseph. Robert stopped the car and those on horses cantered back to see what was going on.

"And the Lord will send his ghosts after us," Chokes said quietly.

The cook may as well have been coming from another planet. None of his companions wanted to acknowledge his words; they did not fit him, it seemed as if a spirit were talking through him.

"What didn't you people tell me that *he* was after you?" Abel continued in a louder voice, fearful, angry.

"We didn't know, Chokes. All I can think is that Jason Starn made a deal with him to track us when we came down here. I should have known he would never forget, even after thirty years."

"Why has Jason Starn been tracking you guys for so long?"

"He is under the impression we stole some silver from him back in '86."

"Did you?"

I could see Joseph struggling not to reveal anything with his face.

"One of us did."

"Who?" Chokes, lowering his voice and looking in turn at the four other men from up north.

"It doesn't matter."

Robert said that and then put the car in gear. The six of them moved on.

A tire went flat and it took a long time to mend it. Abel and Pepe struggled with the tire and tube while the rest of the group looked on. Annie wanted to lend a hand but her guts were aching and there was the beginning of a fever.

"This is not a place for automobiles." The Apache, his tone as dry as the world surrounding them.

"It is a new age, my tacturn friend," Robert, giving their guide a grim smile.

"That it is: A century that will probably see the end of your kind."

"Oh? How do you see that?" Robert, allowing his tone to become patronizing.

The Apache just looked at him for a few moments.

"How do you *not* see it?"

And then he started turning away from the white man. Robert started walking towards him but Isaac put a hand on his arm.

"You're arguing with an Apache."

"I'm not afraid of him."

"It's not a question of being afraid or not being afraid, this is simply a pointless argument. Besides, he is going to lead us to Noah's bones."

The rabbi gave his riding companion a knowing look. Seeing something naked in Robert's eyes, he turned away enough to give his old friend privacy.

"You have to spit out the poison, my friend," Isaac said gently.

"What on earth are you talking about?" Robert asked, offended.

"Spit out the poison, lay down your burden, whatever cliche suits you."

They looked at each other and Robert understood that Isaac understood.

"It's not that simple," the wealthy man said. "As a man of God you should understand that."

Isaac just looked at him.

"I said my peace," he said firmly.

162

46
(1916)

"There is a large group two miles or so down the road," the Apache said. "We should probably avoid them."

He had ridden ahead, disappeared for fifteen minutes, and then returned. He had sped off, leaving us to wonder if he'd return.

"Can we go overland?" Robert asked

"No." Pepe, riding up to where Joseph and the guide were conferring. "We are not supposed to run."

He had been mostly silent the past day; the sound of his voice startled his companions.

"Not *supposed* to run?" Isaac, half listening to Pepe and half trying to figure out if the Apache was planning to lead them into a trap.

"Your car will not make it overland," the Apache said. "You will be very slow on foot and they will overtake you if you turn back."

"So...we're going to meet this party no matter what?"

"Yes."

The four old traveling companions looked at each other. If it was revolutionaries, there was no way they could ungun them. Isaac focused on Pepe.

"What are you seeing?" The rabbi asked.

"What do you mean?"

"I don't know, you almost seem in a trance or something."

"No---"

"And what did you mean by we're not *supposed* to run?"

"Don't listen to me, it's the heat," Pepe tried to smile but his attempt faltered.

"You're a Mexican, you can take this heat better than all of us."

Pepe looked uncomfortable, he reined his horse and rode over to where Chokes sat in the Model T.

"I am sorry; this was only meant for us."

"What are you talking about?" Abel was upset and didn't bother hiding it.

"We redeem ourselves or we die out here or maybe both."

Chokes wanted to protest but he couldn't; he had experienced such things himself and understood all too well.

"I want to be here, Pepe; you're my friend..."

He trailed off searching for words only to understand he had said enough. The Apache tightened the reins and began urging his horse away from the road.

"I will be in the hills watching. If you survive, I will rejoin you and we will continue your quest."

If you survive---aren't you a happy ray of sunshine, the rabbi thought.

Isaac nodded at the Apache who rode off. All of those on horseback surrounded the Ford. A.R. was feeling terrible, as poorly as she would in a Mexican hospital bed forty years later---how was she supposed to stand up with a pistol?

"The Stoic isn't here to save us this time." Joseph, attempting a smile only to have it falter on his face half born.

All of them sat in silence for a couple of minutes, the world around them quiet aside from the insects in some nearby brush. Annie was focused on her pain, it had grown so fierce she couldn't help it. Later she would talk to three of them and learn what they were thinking: At least three of them were cycling through different memories, all from the 1880s when they were young and hadn't experienced flush toilets or lived in place with electric lights. A different world, one they all understood and some of them had moved beyond.

"I took the silver, I am sorry." Pepe speaking to Robert.

"Why? If you needed it, why couldn't you tell us then?"

"I did not think I could pay it back---I was right."

"What was it for?"

"I cannot say, it has to do with my family."

Robert wanted to protest but realized that he had no right.

"I just wish you would have said something," he looked over at Joseph.

The man in the cape gave him a weary smile then turned to look down the road.

"Thirty years," Isaac shook his head. "We leave each far behind in our new lives only to be back here."

"We've never been here before." Robert said softly.

"Not just the place, the situation," the rabbi said impatiently. "I never imagined we'd ride together again; I understood that my memories were mine, but they seemed like another life, that of men who had long since died."

"I feel the same way." Robert, gripping the wheel and then relaxing his hands.

"Me, too." Pepe, looking over at the rifle in the car next to Chokes.

He knew the cook's history, had seen him handle a Winchester---

And Isaac is a crack shot, too. Maybe...

No: There was no *maybe*; if the band was greater than ten men there was no way they stood a chance if they tried to shoot their way out.

"We need to ride on." Isaac said softly.

"Can you say something?" Robert, looking down the road uneasily.

"What do you mean?"

"A prayer or something, you're the man of God here."

"Do you mind if it's in Hebrew?"

"As long as He hears it I don't care if it's in Chinese."

Isaac closed his eyes and began speaking and then chanting in Hebrew. The rest of them made a circle around him that grew as tight as the horses would allow, struck by the music and the beauty of it, the humanity.

If words had tears that would be what it sounds like.

When he finished, the world became silent again---even the insects had stilled and the only sound was the horses breathing and the slow chug of the car engine. Joseph smiled at Isaac who weakly smiled back. The man known as the Cavalier urged his horse down the road and the rest of them followed.

47
(1916)

The world changed in the space of a few minutes--

Coming around a bend the *norteamericanos* found themselves nearly face to face with a group of roughly a hundred men. A couple dozen were on horseback, the rest were on foot---*peons* dragged into the revolution. Annie, who had been feverish, went cold, expecting yelling in Spanish followed by weapons firing bullets into her party. The two groups stared at each other. The leader of the Mexicans was a very brown man, no mustache, battered sombrero. Isaac and Chokes had their hands ready but kept them from their weapons, waiting.

"Lord," the Cavalier said softly. "Lord..."

He trailed off. Isaac was next to him and put the hand that wasn't hovering over his open saddlebag on his friend.

"We have lived a long time, my friend," the rabbi said. "Maybe it is time to go home."

The leader of the Mexicans turned to address his subordinates. He issued a five word command. Before Pepe could translate the Mexicans rode towards the small group from up north and then rode around them, skirting the little group as if they were a snare in a river. Only when the *norteamericanos* were completely surrounded did one of the men on horseback call for his men to stop and ready their arms, the *real* leader. He was somewhere around forty and surprisingly elegant looking with a thin mustache. *El Capitan* approached Robert in the Ford clearly thinking he was the leader.

"Good day." His tone was charming and his English flawless.

"Good day to you." Robert smiled in turn, trying to ignore all the rifles and pistols and shotguns they were surrounded by.

The smile left El Capitan's face when he switched to Spanish.

"Caballeros, ¿Qué les encuentra en este camino que los llevará a su muerte?" Robert recognized the word *muerte* and felt panic setting in---it was no longer a harmless adventure or a "noble quest;" the threat of death suddenly felt very real despite El Capitan's charm and elegant appearance. The rich man looked over at Pepe and saw a reflection of the fear he felt. El Capitan rode over to Harmon's most trusted employee and spoke to him in English. "Who are you, my friend? Why have you brought your companions to a place that will surely mean their deaths?"

"Pepe Gonzales, Capitan." He was looking at the ground out of habit, the days when he was a peon himself. To his old friends, Pepe's bowing and scraping was disconcerting. He had always been a humble man but still a proud one.

"I know many men with that name. *Su ciudad, por favor.*"

"I am from a town called Colina Revantado."

An older peon nearby called out for his Capitan. The leader waved the man over and they conversed in Spanish for nearly a minute. He had short, greasy looking hair and his feet were filthy. The *peon* and Pepe seemed to be recognizing one another.

"What is your full name, Pepe Gonzales?" El Captian appeared suspicious.

"Pepe Gonzales y Rios, Capitan."

El Capitan looked over at the old man and then waved him away.

"Do you recognize Jorge Sanchez? He says you are both from Colina Revantado."

"Yes. It has been a long time, though, more than thirty years."

The Captain sat in his saddle thinking.

"You and your friends are not welcome here; you understand that, right?"

"Yes."

"You understand that nearly all the problems in Mexico come from the north, don't you?"

169

"*Comprende*, Capitán."

He turned to Pepe with a charming yet dangerous smile.

"Then why have the six of you come here?"

"We are here to honor a good friend, Capitan. He saved our lives many years ago and we learned his bones have been left to bleach in the desert. We mean to return them to his family for burial."

This seemed to bewilder and yet please the Captain.

"My...that is both strange and beautiful, Pepe Gonzales y Rios. It would not stop me from having you executed, though."

Isaac listened from nearby. He was at such an angle that he could slip his hand in his saddlebag and pull out his pistol without *El Capitan* seeing it--- not until it was too late.

I was thinking that maybe if I shot him there would be enough confusion that we could get away.

He looked around and saw that most of the men had their weapons, if not pointed at the *gringos*, at the ready.

And then I thought: Who am I kidding?

The Capitan seemed to sense his thoughts and rode over to Isaac.

"You are a rabbi, are you not?"

"Yes, I am."

"Are you here as the moral conscience of the group?" The Capitan studied Isaac's face and the rabbi was startled at how green his eyes were, how alive and intelligent they were.

"No...you are much more than that," the Mexican continued. "I am guessing there is a pistol in that saddlebag---am I correct?"

"Yes."

El Capitan looked pleased.

"I can see you have used that pistol before and I would imagine you are quite effective with it."

"It is not for me to say."

"I like you. I would also imagine that God would like you, as well; a man close to Him who also is not afraid to right wrongs. Please, keep your hands by your sides, rabbi---*por favor*. I would not like for my men to become nervous and shoot you accidentally on purpose."

He turned back to Pepe.

"Jorge tells me of the things you did in your town. Because of this, I am giving you one week. If I see you and your friends where we patrol in eight days, there will be no hesitation in our parts---*comprende?*"

"*Si*, Capitan."

El Capitan smiled and rode over to Joseph.

"You must be the one they call the Cavalier, *el Cabellero*."

"Yes, Capitan. Pleasure to meet you." Joseph touched the brim of his hat.

"I am from the north, a village called Los Huesos. I recall you riding through when I was a boy."

Robert was slightly offended that Joseph was the only one remembered but remained silent.

"To some you were *un payaso* but with your cape you reminded me of a musketeer."

He motioned for his men to continue past the small group as he continued facing the *norteamericanos.*

"Eight days, *el Cabellero*," the Captain smiled. "On that day I will request that a bullet pass through you and bloody your cape."

"Comprende, el capitán."

El Capitan fell in behind his men. Annie's group didn't move as the revolutionaries moved past, they had them pinned in tight. The body odor was astounding, sweat and unwashed clothes and bad breath. Most of the men were impassive, didn't even look at the strangers, but some glared as they walked or rode past. Once the party of six was alone, it was still a few minutes before they could find it in themselves to speak.

"Eight days." Isaac, hands still at his side. Few men had ever scared him, the Captain did.

"We can be out of here in less than that." Joseph, trying to be reassuring but unable to disguise his concern. He could imagine the sensation of a bullet passing through him, maybe fired from the rifle of the man with the greasy hair who knew of Pepe. The Apache appeared out of nowhere.

"The turn off is a mile down the road."

"Why do *you* fear the Mexicans?"

"I do not fear all Mexicans, just the Army."

"That was not the regular army."

The Apache turned and started riding away without answering.

47
(1916)

"I always miss this place when I'm away." The Cavalier, the campfire illuminating the contented expression on his face.

"You're crazy." Robert, cupping his mug full of whiskey.

"To each his own. As for me, I love the open desert."

"See a lot of stars, that's for sure." Chokes, taking the whiskey bottle from Joseph.

The Apache was nearby but outside of the light thrown out by the burning juniper. Forage had been sparse, Joseph and Chokes had ridden an hour to find enough for their fire. Annie's sickness was nearly enough that she considered turning back but worried how she would fare alone. To take her mind off the pain she focused on the voices of her companions and what they did, the depth of the swallows they took off that bottle of whiskey.

"This reminds me of the last time, after the gunfight." Pepe, lost enough in thought that it took him a few moments to realize the bottle was being passed to him. He took it without looking, drank, and then continued.

"You remember? We rode to Los Huesos..." He looked from face to face.

"Yes, we were all terrified," Isaac smiled fondly. "It's a fond memory now and funny that it is."

"You weren't scared, you looked angry." Pepe, handing the bottle to the rabbi.

"I wasn't angry. It's just...I struggle with things."

He wasn't sure if he wanted to elaborate but everyone around the fire was looking at him.

"Every time I shot a man it felt natural," Isaac continued. "I felt no guilt and *that* makes me feel guilty."

"That you have no remorse for killing those men?"

"Yes. The two times on this trip where there could have been shooting, I looked forward to it. If I am honest with myself, I will admit that the idea of being shot to rags does not seem a terrible thing."

He looked from face to face for condemnation or even confusion but only saw the faces of his friends in the sparse light.

"I try, I genuinely do." Isaac spoke so softly it seemed as if he were talking to himself.

"What do you mean?"

"I try to lead a good life, not just one that feels right."

The bottle had come back to him, he drank deeply.

"Are you talking about the expectations of your family?" Joseph, leaning forward and looking concerned.

"No, my expectations for myself. I have always wanted to be a good man---I know you will say that I am a good man but..."

"But our standards are questionable?" Joseph asked, not offended.

"Perhaps, but maybe that's why we rode together in the past and why we ride now." The rabbi looked from face to face again. "Maybe that's why we're friends. Being out here feels right, it makes sense to me. When I am at the temple I am bored a lot of the time. The peculiar thing is, I actually feel closer to God out here---shouldn't it be the opposite?"

"Maybe God always intended for you to be an outlaw."

"How could that be?" Isaac almost looked offended. "Why would God want me on such a dark path?"

Joseph just shrugged. The bottle was in Pepe's hands again.

"How did thirty years get by so fast?"

"And those days pass faster all the time," Chokes nodded.

Joseph was looking somewhere none of his companions could see. He was staring in the fire but seeing past it, falling in. Something none of the others could identify was coming off him in waves, probably some sort of pain.

They kept waiting for him to shake it, smile, and say *I'm not going to let this nonsense get me down*, but he wasn't coming back. A minute passed, then two.

"I can't let it go," he said, a tremor in his voice.

Pepe tried to hand Joseph the bottle but the older man shook his head.

"It's like what you said about nostalgia, Isaac; it's all I have. I just remember the fun of it all, those months we rode together. Even after I lost you fellows, I couldn't stop, I still can't. I am too old now, too old for getting a normal job---and I don't want one. I want this," he gestured at the fire and his friends and then more widely at the surrounding wilderness. "I will be 61 in June living the life of a man forty years younger. I can't hack it anymore, but I still want it."

"Settling down isn't all it's cracked up to be." Isaac shook his head and took the bottle from Pepe.

"I understand what you said about dying out here, I've been thinking about that since we crossed the border, maybe since I decided we needed to find the bones."

Joseph caught himself, how morbid he was becoming. His companions were all looking at him with concern and some awkwardness; he was making them uncomfortable and bringing them down.

"Golly." He struggled for a moment but then the smile came. It felt strange on his face but he felt obliged to wear it. "Sorry, fellows," Joseph forced a chuckle. "Didn't mean to trudge down such a shadowed road."

Isaac handed the bottle to him and he took it. There wasn't much left.

"Kill it, it's yours." Pepe, still feeling awkward.

Joseph looked over to Robert who raised his cup.

"To the four of us," Robert proposed. "And our new friends Abel and A.R.."

"Hear, hear," The Cavalier chuckled.

175

He raised the bottle, drank, and then looked up at the stars.

48
(1916)

"I miss my eggs--you can do so much with 'em," the cook sighed.

Sadly for Chokes there weren't any eggs in that part of the desert. Instead, there was oatmeal.

"I hate oatmeal: Hate eating it, hate cleaning the pan afterward," he scowled.

The rest of the party said nothing when he dished it up but he saw their faces: *Oatmeal--again? Why can't a man who earns his living as a cook make decent oatmeal?*

"This makes me think about those repairs on Mr. Harmon's house." Pepe, using his spoon more to stir than to eat with.

"How so?" Chokes asked.

"I think this would make an excellent spackle."

Isaac and Joseph laughed and Chokes eventually joined in. Robert ate alone sitting in the car, occasionally looking over at his companions. He did not desire their company.

After breakfast, they packed up and continued down the rough road. Annie was doing her best to keep the pain to herself. It showed on her face, though. When she got questions of concern the teenager mentioned *lady troubles* and that would stop all inquiries in their tracks.

As always, Robert's thoughts drifted off as Chokes talked non-stop about everything, anything, and nothing. To Robert, it was just a blur of words. *I kept thinking about the previous night, the woe Joseph shared with us. I have never been able to respect a weak man nor a pathetic man and he was both. He seemed on the verge of tears and I wanted to bash his eyes in.*

When the party took a break a few hours later he couldn't even look Joseph in the face. The other man picked up on it and confronted him.

"Why are you such a sour man, Bob?"

Robert met his gaze. The others formed around them in a loose circle aside from the Apache who was watching some birds.

"Better a sour man than a wretched man, I imagine."

"You see me as wretched?"

"God, man---who wouldn't? Sixty years old and no real prospects, sleeping in parks in a shabby cape. If that is not wretched I have no idea what is."

Isaac and Pepe looked away, the latter shaking his head. When Joseph spoke, his voice was quiet but firm.

"For years I have tried to determine why you dislike me. Maybe it was because you thought I stole from our group but now we know I didn't and the loathing still continues: I think I know why."

Isaac turned back towards the two men and put his hand on Joseph's shoulder.

"Joe, let it go---"

Joseph didn't seem to see him, he was focused on Robert with a fierceness in his eyes.

"I always accepted you. I saw who you are, who you really are, and I accepted you. I think you dislike yourself as a man so much, any man who knows you and still accepts you is someone not to be trusted."

Robert just looked at him. In his mind he had been preparing to rail against Joseph and the life he lead and his stupid cape but---

The words were gone. It was as if what Joseph had said were acid that had been thrown on them and eaten them away. The older man was not done with him.

"Yes, I am shabby, Robert. Very true I have no prospects, but I lead my own life and I lead it proudly. How about you?"

The four old friends just looked at one another. After nearly a minute the Apache walked over.

"We're wasting time. You can kill each other after we find your friend."

"How far away are we?" Isaac, wondering if it was possible Joseph and Robert would come to blows.

"Two hours, maybe three. Depends on how many times you stop to argue."

The road got worse with each mile, the tracks in the hard ground fainter and fainter.

"It's like people just died out here the way the road is fading."

Joseph said that without thinking and then realized the effect that would have on morale.

"We must be close," he added before addressing their guide. "Tell us about when you found the bones."

The Apache said nothing for a few moments.

"I was out looking for something, I found your friend instead."

"What were you looking for?"

"You asked about when I found the bones, I told you."

"What you were looking for was very personal, I take it."

"You take it correctly."

"So, you picked up his gun belt and traded in."

"Yes."

Joseph smiled at the Apache and stopped talking out of respect.

"You can start collecting," the guide said a few moments later.

"Pardon?"

The Apache pointed under some scrub. Joseph dropped off his horse and got on his hands and knees to find what the Indian had seen: A leg bone. He didn't want to touch it, doing so seemed disrespectful somehow. Isaac had no such qualms and gently picked the bone up to study it. The others gathered around, taken by the fact they were staring at the bone of someone they had known, someone that had just been alive as they were. Annie was relieved; soon they could leave the wilderness and could help her find a doctor.

"There are more bones, unless you just need one as a souvenir."

"Yes," Isaac said, pointing all around with the Stoic's leg bone. "Perhaps we could all go in a different direction and gather them."

"I'll get out a sack to put them in." Chokes, nodding and walking towards the car.

There must have been something wild and hungry out there because the bones had been scattered a couple hundred feet in each direction. There were chew marks on some of the bones but the old men decided to ignore that. The rib cage was intact and half buried in the grit. All five men gathered around it.

"It's too big to go in the sack."

"Yes, I think we have enough bones to offer him a proper internment."

"But the ribs...that is where the heart was."

Joseph said that then looked over at Robert who remained silent.

The ribs...that is where the heart is.

The rich man considered Noah's death and wondered what had happened to his heart; the world was suddenly that much more cruel and even more complicated than it had been a minute earlier.

"Maybe we can't take it, but we can do a toast or something."

"Excellent idea."

Chokes got a bottle of whiskey out of the back of the car. The Apache came over to where the men had gathered and got off his horse.

"You have found your friend, my work is done."

"You're welcome to stay the night if you like."

"No. I just need my money."

Robert called over to Chokes to bring the three hundred pesos when he brought the whiskey.

"Sorry you have to leave, you seem like a good man." Joseph, not sure he meant what he was saying. Seeing the indifference in the Apache's eyes he continued. "I am also sorry you hate us. Not all of us mistreated Indians." The Apache looked at him, ignoring Chokes who had walked over with the money.

"Leave us to our death," the guide said quietly yet firmly.

"I don't understand---"

"No, you don't."

He took the money, got on his horse, and rode off.

The ribs were next to a cluster of scrub. Instead of gathering firewood, Pepe lit the bushes and they gathered around to pass the bottle. No words were spoken at first, all words seemed meaningless and small. Pepe looked at the ribs and remembered during the gunfight, how terrified he had been and how guilty had felt about the possibility of leaving his wife and small children without a husband and father---

And then the Stoic had appeared---*El Hombre*---and had saved them with a speed and skill that seemed almost inhuman. After the gunfight, they had thanked him which the Stoic had acknowledged with a nod---expect for Robert: There had been a nod and a smile; Pepe had been thinking about that smile for nearly thirty years. Robert was looking at the bones but his face revealed nothing. Instead of passing the bottle he had poured some in a cup as he had the night before.

"Do we know where to deliver them?" Joseph, kneeling to examine the ribs.

"I believe he had people in the Denver area."

Joseph got up and faced Robert.

"Would you mind seeking them out for all of us?"

181

Robert looked up at the Cavalier, for once there was no anger or hatred or bitterness, all of his companions saw it.

"It would be my pleasure."

There was no reconciliation between them, just an agreement on one matter and one matter only.

49
(1916)

The next morning's sun lit a pain inside each of them with a peculiar fire. There had been a second bottle of whiskey and a vicious burst of wind that had moved the fire and charred the bones. The memory would come back only when Isaac spotted the blackened ribs.

"We sent him off well, I think."

"Yes, his people will send him off in a more Christian way, I assume."

Robert knelt next to the bones despite all the aches in his body.

"I don't know if this matter will ever be settled."

"What do you mean?"

"Something tells me he was murdered. Those Mexicans back in the town seemed to think a Mormon did it."

"Did it ever occur to you that maybe they wanted to stir things up?" Isaac, shaking his head and then regretting the movement. "Whites versus whites, us whites kill each other off?"

"It rings true." Robert stood up and looked east, over lands they had yet to travel.

"If we are here in seven days we will be shot."

"I am not saying this matter can be settled at this time."

It was easy to see that the words were the product of some private but deep grief and a couple of the others simply nodded before going back to packing their things up. Robert poured the rest of his coffee next to the bones. Annie was unable to even take care of her bedroll and was relieved that she no longer had to hide her infirmity.

"Are you ill, A.R.? I mean, do you think it's more than *the curse*?" Joseph asked.

Pepe looked over and then Chokes.

"I thought it was a flu at first but I think I need a doctor, I hurt real bad."
"Could be your appendix," Robert looked anxious. "We will get you to a hospital as soon as possible."

The small party followed the crude track back through the grit and scrub. An hour after leaving camp, Isaac felt *something*. He had always been the first one to pick up danger when they had ridden in the past.
I thought it was the Mexicans, that they had decided eight days was too generous or maybe some of the group had disagreed with their captain.
Another group was emerging from an arroyo maybe half a mile to the south. There were ten men led by the Holy Man, Isaac could sense him before he could see him. The Cavalier held his hand up for his companions to stop and wait. The others looked at him with uncertainty and he just shook his head.
"We can't outrun them, we may as well wait to see what they want."
"They probably want to rob us." Pepe, looking around with growing anxiety.
"No, I don't think that's it." Isaac, debating whether to pull his revolver from the saddle bag.
Ten of them and us with four guns and two men who can use them well. I knew you could shoot, A.R., but you were clearly out of the fight. I wondered if, after all the years that had passed, if that was the time for us to go down shooting.
"I don't mind dying out here." Robert, his tone unreadable.
"I thought you hated it out here, so far from indoor plumbing and decent restaurants."
"I do. I just know who they are and that they will never let us be."
Chokes, quiet and focused for once, reached down for his rifle.
"They probably figured we came back to dig up the silver we stole," Isaac, giving Pepe a rueful look.
"*Yo dije que lo sentía,*" the Mexican said tersely.

A few seconds later the smaller group had been surrounded.. Stern's men were all hard faced, experienced looking hands in their thirties and forties. Isaac recognized the oldest one as a survivor of the gunfight in Deming.

He had been gut shot, I saw the pain on his face. Back then, you could die from that but he had been young and strong enough to pull through.

The Holy Man rode up to Joseph with a tight smile. As to why he had approached them without his men the first time Annie only had theories so wild and fearful she could never share them.

"Good day, Joseph," the Holy Man chuckled. "Beautiful morning, isn't it?"

"It was. To what do we owe this pleasure."

"I believe you know."

"The silver is gone, has been gone for thirty years."

"Where did it go?"

"It doesn't matter, it is gone."

The Holy Man just looked at him for a few seconds.

"Well, we can't have ridden this way for nothing; guess we'll have to kill you."

"What do you gain from such a thing?"

The ageless man with the cruel smile looked in Joseph's eyes. An understanding was exchanged.

"Dear Lord," Joseph whispered.

"What?" Isaac, his hand in his saddlebag.

One of the men on horseback, a small man with a tremendous mustache, caught the movement and brought his rifle up. The Cavalier had his own pistol in the back of his trousers, concealed by the cape everyone tended to ridicule.

Before I am shot to ribbons I will put a bullet in his forehead, see if he can be killed.

And then a noise came down the arroyo, dozens of men. The ones on horseback led with the ones on foot jogging behind them: El Capitan and his men. The Holy Man turned to the man with the tremendous mustache who had been fixing to shoot Isaac.

"Hold them the best you can. I will let Mr. Starn know of your actions and your families will be compensated."

Mr. Mustache looked from the Holy Man to the Mexicans and was clearly unsure which party to be more fearful of.

"Will do."

The Holy Man looked each of the six in the face and said a number to each of them in turn before riding off. Annie would not recall the numbers he gave her companions, only that hers was "41."

The ten gunmen turned to face the charging Mexicans. The oldest of them, the survivor from Deming, didn't seem pleased.

"The boss is gone," a man with a beat up, blue hat mewled. "We should just lay our arms down."

"Them Mexicans will kill us whether we fight or not," one of his companions said. "Reckon we may as well send a few of 'em to Hell."

"I've been shot, it's the Devil's own misery," the first one replied.

"It'll be over soon." Mr. Mustache was trying to sound tough, but his voice was shaky.

He brought his rifle up and began firing. His companions, some reluctantly, joined suit and the Mexicans returned fire. The smallest group took cover, most just flattening on the ground as a gun battle took place all around them. It hurt Annie like fury to get off her horse, to move at all. She tried to distract herself in the worst way possible, remembering the Holy Man as he looked at her and said that number: *41*.

Ten minutes later all of Joseph Starn's men lay dead or dying. The Capitan rode up and singled Isaac out.

"Two or three of them have not passed. Maybe you could offer them some comfort."

"They were here to kill us, Capitan."

"They are just men, you are a man of God."

"Perhaps, but would they want the words of a rabbi?"

"They would probably take reassurances from any man of God at this point."

Isaac walked over to the first of the men on the ground, it was the older man who had survived the battle in Deming. His face was contorted in agony, the pain was clenching him so all he could do was wheeze.

"Damn Mexicans shot me in the same place in my innards."

Isaac knelt beside him.

"God will find you and forgive you. Be at peace, go home to God."

The man just muttered an obscenity. The Captain had been standing nearby. He drew his pistol and motioned for Isaac to step away.

"Please, I do not wish to get blood on you."

The rabbi moved away. There was a single shot and the man's suffering ended.

Three men were dispatched in that manner and then the Captain called for his men to get back into formation.

"Are we just going to leave these men out here?" Isaac, looking around at the bodies.

"What do you think they would have done with you?" The Captain saw something he liked and smiled. "You really are a man of God. If you and your friends like you can bury these men, but we have to ride on."

"Thank you for saving us, *El Capitan*."

The smile left the Mexican's face.

"Six days, *el Caballero*."

"I thought we had seven left."

187

"One day is the price of us saving you."

He touched the brim of his hat, and led his men down the road.

Two hours later the party of six was back at the fork in the road; turning north would take our party back towards the border. A man on horseback was coming from that direction. As he got closer we could make out his white hair and mustache. The man touched the brim of his hat as he approached.

"Good morning. I am surprised to see other gringos in these parts," he said.

Something was familiar about the man, Isaac decided.

"Excuse me, but you look like the writer Ambrose Bierce," he said.

The man laughed and his mirth brought on a coughing fit.

"I am him and, as you can tell, I have seen better days."

Isaac rode his horse closer to the older man.

"I heard you disappeared down in Mexico."

Bierce appeared pleased by that.

"It would appear the news was right for once."

"Where are you riding to?" The Cavalier asked.

"Wherever," Bierce shrugged. "Possibly to join Villa and ride with him to glory, more likely to be executed against a wall and left to become another pile of bones in the desert."

"We are heading back to New Mexico." Robert said.

"Well, then I will wish you a good day, gentlemen," the older writer touched his hat.

"Would you accept a traveling companion?" The Cavalier asked.

The other four men looked at Joseph.

"If the Captain finds you here in six days---" Isaac warned.

"I know." Joseph smiled at the rabbi, his best friend.

Robert wasn't listening. The truth was, he didn't care. He wanted to get back across the border.

"There is nothing for me back there." Joseph frowned. "Nothing in the United States, nothing in 1916."

"Hear, hear," Ambrose Bierce, sipping from a flask.

Joseph looked over at each of his companions in turn.

"Thank you for coming with me on this final adventure of ours. Now, you will go north and I will go south."

"Don't be a fool. This is not a jape, you will be killed."

Robert yelled that, clearly agitated. Gripping the wheel then relaxing his hands only to grip the wheel again.

"Isaac and I will help you," he continued. "Make sure you have a decent life."

"What? So I can have another heart attack in another city? So I can feel trapped and miserable surrounded by crowds and motorcars?"

Robert averted his eyes.

"Thank you, though," Joseph continued. "You find Noah's people, I bet a lot of the weight you're carrying will be gone."

The wealthy man looked down, taking his hands of the wheel, removing his hat, and turning it over in his hands.

"I don't know, I think it has become a part of me," Robert said.

Joseph nodded over at Isaac who smiled.

"Come back and see me when you're done down here," the rabbi said uncomfortably.

Joseph just touched the brim of his hat and then went to Annie. Through her suffering a deep sadness came up like a mighty bird coming over a ridge. That was the last time she was going to see him, the girl knew that.

"Don't look sad, A.R., this is the best I could ever hope for."

"I just wish I could keep riding with you."

The girl looked down at the neck of her horse, embarrassed by the tears that came despite her best efforts. Forty-one years later she could still see the sweet smile on his face, all the love; it was more love than anyone had ever sent her way or ever would.

And then he was next to his new traveling companion. The two men instantly engaged in a conversation as they moved off slowly down the road. The group from the north, now five, watched until their voices became too faint to hear and their shapes too small to see.

We are never going to see him again, are we?

Isaac, his voice so soft only Pepe could hear him. Even after forty-one years Annie can still see the hurt on his face. The girl nearly died before they reached a Mexican hospital and then nearly died when they had her open; A.R.'s appendix burst as the doctor was about to take it out. That was the second to last time she was in a hospital room.

Annie was not fit to travel for weeks. She contemplated going back to Mexico to find the Cavalier. In the end she was more pragmatic than she gave herself credit for because that romantic notion was easily dismissed. Also, A.R. understood that she would not find the Cavalier or his new friend, not alive, at least. When she returned several years later Annie asked around and would continue to ask around the rest of her life. No one ever fessed up to knowing the fate of either Ambrose Bierce or her dear friend the Cavalier.

50
(2008)

Abuelo had stopped talking, the words had just grown quieter and quieter until the older man stopped talking altogether and his grandson respectfully let a deep silence take control of the room.

"She told us that," Hector said quietly. "And she asked for some water."

He looked over at the painting and attempted to covertly wipe a tear away; his *nieto* pretended not to see.

"Esmerelda started crying," the old doctor continued softly. "I guess you will not think less of me if I admit that I joined in the tears with your grandmother."

He walked closer to the painting and his grandson joined him.

"This painting," the older man explained. "Is of the small, poor *pueblo* known as *Los Huesos*."

"You had it done after all of Annie's stories?"

Hector did not speak for nearly a minute.

"That was part of it."

He motioned to the couch, both men walked over and sat on the chair facing each other.

"You never knew your great-grandfather, nieto, and I am glad for that. He was a mean man, very petty and cruel."

Hector looked over at the painting.

"When I was fifteen I was tired of his meanness, so I hit him very hard with a metal pipe."

Reuben gasped, he couldn't help it, his abuelo had always been a gentle man. "Did it kill him?"

"No, but I knew to run away from the town I had grown up in."

He looked over at the painting and then at his grandson. Slowly, Reuben was beginning to understand. Hector took both his *nieto's* hands in his own and looked back at the painting.

"And now I have told my story, and now I can rest."

Written between 20 April, 2015 and 8 February, 2021

www.ingramcontent.com/pod-product-compliance
Lightning Source LLC
Chambersburg PA
CBHW051957220626
47052CB00004B/975